TIME GHOST

Books by the same author

The Dragon Fire Trilogy:
Jet Smoke and Dragon Fire
Into the Spiral
The Shining Bridge

Billy's Drift

TIME GHOST

CHARLES ASHTON

WALKER BOOKS

AND SUBSIDIARIES

LONDON • BOSTON • SYDNEY

Time Ghost *was intended as a*
small tribute to the author of
Tom's Midnight Garden, *Philippa Pearce.*
It is dedicated to two Strangers who
turned up as I was in the process of
writing it, and whose arrival affected
Miss Pearce and myself in
a somewhat similar fashion:
Nat Christie-Norland and
Gudrun Ashton-Roy;
though naturally one mustn't forget
their respective Retinues,
Sally and Ben, Rachel and Charlie.
To Charlie Roy I am also indebted for
the title of my story, which he dredged
up with the aid of a very unreliable
German-English dictionary.

First published 2000 by Walker Books Ltd
87 Vauxhall Walk, London SE11 5HJ

2 4 6 8 10 9 7 5 3 1

Text © 2000 Charles Ashton
Jacket illustration © 2000 Julek Heller

This book has been typeset in Sabon.

Printed and bound in Great Britain by
Creative Print and Design (Wales), Ebbw Vale

British Library Cataloguing in Publication Data
A catalogue record for this book is
available from the British Library.

ISBN 0-7445-5945-6

CONTENTS

MAY'S SON

"I'm going to play chess with Robert," Maudie announced.

"Oh," said Olly, "is that why you don't have any clothes on?"

"I've got clothes on!"

Olly pretended to peer closely at his sister. "Oh yes," he said, "I can see them now."

He got a sharp rap on the head from Maudie's knuckles. "We're playing it out in the garden – nerd," she said, "and in case you hadn't noticed, it's a lovely day, so I'll be sunbathing at the same time. *That's* all."

"Oh – right," Olly said sarcastically. Everyone knew Maudie fancied their cousin like mad, and that was the real reason for her state of undress. Olly half wondered if he would join them and they could have a tournament; it might be worth it, just to cheese Maudie off. But he didn't like Robert all that much, and he

7

was even less keen on the thought of spending a whole afternoon watching Maudie making big eyes at him.

It was a bit of a disaster of an afternoon. Uncle Marty had been supposed to be taking them to the beach but his car had broken down again, and besides, he was doing some sort of job for Aunt Rosie which he hadn't got finished in time. Olly felt he really needed to get away somewhere. But where?

That was when he thought of the old bike in the damp, stone-flagged garage. It was Aunt Rosie's bike – Great-Aunt Rosemary, that was – and it had definitely seen better days.

But although the tyres were both flat, there was a pump which still worked, and the tyre rubber didn't seem to be perished. Olly gave each tyre seventy pumps, then stood up sweatily – and banged his head against the angled section of the ceiling where the loft stairs went up. Old plaster showered into his hair and down his T-shirt. He did a crouching, head-clutching dance round the garage floor till his head felt a bit better, then went back and punched the ceiling, sending down a second shower of broken plaster onto the bike.

He rubbed his knuckles and gazed at the small hole in the plaster. He had laid the laths bare, parallel strips of dusty wood that looked too pale because they had never seen the light, and between them blackness: the dark interior of the wall.

It was strange. Somehow he never thought of the garage and the loft as connected places. The loft, which you got into by climbing a staircase from the path outside, had three rooms full of junk – old furniture, old crockery, old books in a wormed bookshelf, three old drawers where Aunt Rosie stored her apples. Olly squinted up between the uncovered laths, trying to see into the loft. But all he could see was blackness – apart from something he could make out only vaguely: a right-angled something. The corner of a piece of wood, or maybe a book which had slipped down the inside of the wall.

There was plaster everywhere: in his hair, down his jeans, on the bicycle chain, and it took him a while to get rid of it all. Then he swung his leg over the bike and pushed off.

He didn't know anyone in Rothes, and no one knew him, so it didn't matter who saw him on this cronk. It was like taking a trip back into the past: once upon a time everyone rode about on old fossils like Aunt Rosie's bike – all black, no gears, no transfers, no logos, no plastic casings, solid steel mudguards. Aunt Rosie's had a decrepit wicker basket attached to the handlebars. But it ran surprisingly smooth. Aunt Rosie had got it when she was a student, nearly seventy years ago.

He stood at the top of the road between

Rothes and Edenbridge. He was pouring with
sweat, his heart thundering. The day was clear
as well as hot, and the whole country seemed
to have opened up around him. To the east
was the deep blue line of the North Sea, and to
the west he thought he could have seen right
across Scotland, if his sight had been good
enough, and even caught a glimpse of the roof
of his own house away on the edge of Glasgow. The road split just over the top of the hill,
the main road running invitingly off downhill
towards Edenbridge, while a smaller road
wound along the ridge in the direction of Hill
of Service with its round green top. Olly
wished he had brought a bottle of water, or at
least an apple. He pushed off along the smaller
road. If he had coasted down to Edenbridge,
he would only have had to toil back uphill
again, but the unknown road was more level.

It wound in and out of corners, between
heat-radiating stone walls or under stretches
of shady trees. Rothes sank away out of sight
in the folds of the green fields. It was very
quiet.

Olly saw the tower, squat and dark grey
above the trees, just before he saw the
National Trust sign announcing *Scotservice
Tower, open 10 a.m. to 5 p.m.* beside a dusty
track. He knew you would probably have to
pay to get in and he had no money, but he
thought he would go along and look anyway.

There was something he liked about the plain, square building. Perhaps it looked cool in the shimmering heat. At any rate, there seemed plenty of trees about, and that meant shade.

There were three cars in a dusty carpark, and a sign that read *Adults £2, Concessions 50p. Grounds free.* Free grounds was better than nothing. Olly dismounted and left the bike on the grass at the edge of the carpark, and then walked off in the direction of a sign marked *Nature Trail.*

The woods round Scotservice Tower were wonderfully cool. A can of juice or an ice cream and they would have been perfect. The trees were large and well spaced, and the soft path he went on was solemn and stately.

But Olly must have taken a wrong turning, because he soon came to a part of the wood where people obviously didn't go much. The trees here were smaller and untidier. He went down into a small dip across a crushed-down wire fence and the path faded out altogether. He hesitated, then continued uphill through a forest of tall willowherb where a large space among the trees was opening up.

Here the sun beat down on him again, and Olly was just about to turn back to the wood shade when the air suddenly filled with whirring and flapping. Startled, he looked up. It was as though someone had shaken the trees and filled the air with a black dandruff of crows. Now they were whirring and winnowing round and round the edge of the clearing.

He noticed a grey wall up ahead of him over the green spikes of the willowherb. It was not the wall of Scotservice Tower: it had a greenish, derelict look to it. He pushed on, trying to ignore the crows.

A ruined house, as he had guessed. The crows whirred and wheeled, and the ruined house lay silent, shadowy somehow even in the full sunlight.

He got no further than seeing that it was a pretty large, long house, and that most of its roof was gone except for a squat round turret-shaped bit at this end, when a sharp shout made him jump and set the crows off into a fresh flurry.

A man appeared, waving his arms and running towards him. He shouted several more times and then stopped, still waving his arms. He was just near enough for Olly to see that he was a large, untidy, unshaven sort of man, and that he had a vacant look about him.

The man shouted again, and Olly understood that he was not wanted. "No!" the voice came, both angry and complaining. "No! Private! Go away! It's private!"

Olly mumbled, "I'm sorry," and immediately turned back into the willowherb. The voice followed him as he pushed his way back down the slope. "Go away! Go away!" The crows circled over the treetops, round and round, clattering their wings against the leaves. Olly crossed back over the crushed fence. He was walking fast, panting slightly. He had not meant any harm. It had said the grounds were free; there was nothing about private, and crows, and lumbering nutters. He didn't want to spend any longer in this place.

The sound of the crows faded behind him. From the treetops above his head there came a muted *caaa!* from a last outrider. The silence must have been pretty well complete after that, because Olly even heard the very faint fluttering in the leaves when, a couple of seconds later, a something – a white something moving against the background of the forest shadow – came rocking down and floated to the ground just in front of him.

Automatically, he bent and picked it up. It was a scrap of stiff-seeming paper, slightly curved, not flat, rather browned and tattered at the edges. There was handwriting on both sides of it. He made out the word *combination,* but the writing was faint.

He continued on his way, the scrap of paper slipped gently between two of his fingers. He almost threw it away when he got back to the carpark, because his mind was still more on the crows and the ruin and the shouting man, but at the last moment he dropped it into the basket at the front of the bike.

*   *   *

Two hot hours later, Olly was back at Burn-side House. Robert had beaten Maudie four times at chess, and she was in a very bad mood and needed her younger brother for a proper quarrel. By the time they had finished quar-relling, it was time for their evening meal, and Maudie could blame Olly for the state of her emotions when she slammed upstairs and refused to come and eat.

"That girl's not right in the head," Aunt Rosie remarked, as she often did about Maudie.

"What's wrong with her?" Uncle Marty enquired.

"Robert kept beating her at chess," Olly informed him.

"You didn't! Could you not have let her win – just once?" Uncle Marty asked.

Robert bristled. "Look, Dad," he said. "In the real world, people compete. You know? There's winners and there's losers. I like being a winner, OK?"

"Hey, peace, man," Uncle Marty said mildly, holding his hands up palm outwards to his son. "I'll try and bear that in mind." Uncle Marty still lived back in the Sixties, when, he said, all the best people had been hippies. He had only had his hair cut twice in the past thirty years and, from the look of it, had never brushed it once.

Aunt Rosie, who was used to his strange looks and strange ideas, tried to calm everyone down by saying, "Things'll be better when Lucy comes." In fact everyone knew Maudie and Lucy were more likely simply to ignore each other.

Robert and Lucy's parents – Uncle Marty and Auntie Cath, that was – didn't live together any more, since Auntie Cath had got fed up with Uncle Marty never having any money. Robert and Lucy lived with Auntie Cath most of the time, but would go to stay with Uncle Marty in his small flat in Edenbridge some weekends. If they came to see him for longer periods they would stay with their granny – Aunt Rosie, that was – as she had so much more room at Burnside House.

Aunt Rosie wanted to know where Olly had got to on her bike. She was worried that the tyres wouldn't have stayed up and was quite surprised to hear that they had.

"But I hit my head on that bit in the garage," Olly admitted, "and some plaster fell off." He thought it was better not to mention punching the ceiling.

Aunt Rosie said it was time the garage was re-plastered, and Uncle Marty said he would see to it. Everyone knew it wouldn't be done for years.

Olly recounted his visit to Scotservice Tower and described the ruined house and the man. "How was I to know it was private?" he finished. "There wasn't any sign out."

"That would be Miglo Hall," Uncle Marty smiled. "And old Ronnie. The Sharpes, down at Lower Service, let him stay up there in his caravan."

"I didn't see any caravan," Olly said.

Uncle Marty laughed. "That's right – it's sitting right inside the old house! It's a really damp place for a caravan, but – you know? It's what he wants. He likes his privacy."

Aunt Rosie said, "He was May's son, you know."

Olly knew who May was, but all the stories about her were of a young woman. It was funny to think of her as the mother of an old man. May had died years ago. "Is he all right?" he asked. "I mean, is he kind of – normal?"

Uncle Marty shrugged. "I mean, man – what's normal?" he said, and started to roll himself a cigarette.

"Hippy," Robert muttered, though Uncle Marty didn't seem to hear.

Aunt Rosie grunted. "Poor old Ronnie," she said. "We used to know him very well, of course. We used to push him around in our old pram when he was a baby. He was always a bit strange. No, there was definitely a couple of slates loose. He started taking *turns* as well, when he grew up. I'm surprised he hasn't

killed himself up there, all on his own in that
caravan. He would fall down and knock
things over when he had one of his turns. He's
a big man. He knocked a lamp over and set fire
to the Cottage once, but of course May was
still alive then, so she got it put out in good
time."

"The Sharpes look out for him," Uncle
Marty said. Then he suddenly added, "I could
take you to visit him, Olly!"

"I don't want to visit him!" Olly burst out.
"That place gave me the creeps!"

"It's family history, man," Uncle Marty
said. "Your granny and your Aunt Rosie used
to play there."

Aunt Rosie had the faraway look that
always came over her face when she was thinking of the past. "Yes," she said, "we used to
play in the tower. We rented a house from the
Hopes for a year after we sold Lingerton – just
before we moved to Rothes. The tower was
derelict then, but it was full of old things, a
wonderful place. I remember there was a suit
of armour, and we used to put the helmet on.
I think it was Chinese, or Arabian or something of the sort. The Hopes used to travel a
lot in the East. I can always remember that suit
of armour particularly."

MAY'S TREE

Later, Olly thought about Uncle Marty's strange offer of taking him to meet old Ronnie.

He wasn't sure he liked Uncle Marty much, but that might have been because his mum and dad never said anything nice about him. When Mum called Uncle Marty a hippy she meant it as a serious insult.

Olly lay in the lumpy old iron bed and stared up at the sloping ceiling above him, and tried to forget about both Uncle Marty and old Ronnie. He was in one of the attic bedrooms, which were hardly ever used now and were filled with an old, sad, deserted feel. Through the small skylight window he could see a single star in the not-quite-dark eastern sky.

There was always this feeling about the past at Aunt Rosie's house. It wasn't just because Aunt Rosie was always telling stories about bygone days. Perhaps it was because she had lived here for almost her whole life. Things around her had changed – and yet somehow nothing changed. Like the way she still called the next-door house "the Cottage" – that was typical. It had once belonged to Burnside House, but Aunt Rosie had sold it because she got fed up with all the bad tenants who lived there after May Forester and her son left. Sometimes she even called it "May's cottage", though May hadn't lived in it for over fifty years. The sign beside its front door quite clearly said *May Cottage*, however, and there was now a thick lonicera hedge between its garden and Aunt Rosie's.

Olly started thinking about Lingerton, the farm where the twins, Rosemary and Olive – Aunt Rosie and his own grandmother, that was – had grown up. You could see Lingerton out of the skylight window, except that the old buildings were hidden behind a large grey modern shed. Everyone knew the story of how they had had to leave Lingerton when Great-Grandfather Martin McClay died, how Great-Grandmother Jane had had to sell the farm and how she and the twins had come to Rothes and bought Burnside House. The twins had been thirteen then, and Aunt Rosie had lived in Burnside House ever since – over seventy years. Grandmother Olive had not; she had died thirty years before Olly was born.

Did he like being at Burnside House? He

wasn't sure. He and Maudie had been sent over for the summer holidays because their parents couldn't afford a family holiday that year, because of the double-glazing.

Lucy arrived, and unexpectedly she and Maudie became the best of friends. That meant that Olly and Robert saw more of each other, especially since Maudie now practically stopped talking to Robert. She would still honour Olly with a few fond names now and then – like "little jerk", "big ears", "scumbag" – or with pieces of gentle sisterly advice like "See this stick, Olly? If you come in here again I'll push it right down your throat till it comes out in your pants". On the whole, Olly got a quieter life if he stuck around with Robert.

The boys spent the afternoon with Uncle Marty when he finally got round to sorting his car. In Uncle Marty's case, sorting the car meant standing gazing under the bonnet for long stretches of time, shaking his head sadly, and now and again running an oil-blackened hand through a tangle of his long hair, which was supposed to be tied back but had come out and kept flopping over his face. It was Olly who noticed the wire which was hanging off, and when Uncle Marty attached it again, the engine started immediately. He hooted with glee and called Olly a genius, and Olly modestly murmured, "It was only a bit of wire," but he felt pleased with himself all the same.

"We should give her a run, just to see everything's all right," Uncle Marty said in the evening, and both boys felt it was their right and their duty to go with him.

They drove out of Rothes towards Bleachfield, then off into a maze of small twisting roads. Finally they turned off onto a farm track and ground and bumped their way up a hill for a little, then turned and came to a stop at a quiet farm close.

There was something old-fashioned about this farm. It didn't seem to have any big modern buildings, like the grey shed at Lingerton. The buildings were dull reddish stone, with saggy slate roofs. Bulging wooden walls were propped with sticks, and one shed with a rusty tin roof looked as though it would simply have fallen down if it hadn't been completely stuffed with pale green bales of new hay.

"I have to do some haggling with Jim Sharpe, boys," Uncle Marty said as he swung the car door open. "Hope that's all right. Come on in with me."

Olly got out and had started to follow Uncle Marty when he realized that Robert was still sitting in the car. He stopped, hesitating, and that made Uncle Marty stop too and ask what the matter was.

"Oh, I forgot," he said, when Olly told him

21

Robert wasn't coming, "he's got a thing about the Sharpes, you know? He doesn't like them much. Come on, it doesn't have to stop you coming. You haven't met any real farming folk, have you?"

Olly felt torn. It was true; being from Glasgow he hadn't met any farming people, but he wasn't really sure he wanted to. He thought this farm had a spooky feel. He also thought Robert would be offended if he left him in the car. On the other hand, Uncle Marty might be offended if he didn't go into the house. Olly was caught in the middle.

"It's up to you, kiddo," Uncle Marty said breezily, and turned to go on. Olly turned this way and that, finally decided to go back to the car, then found his feet had taken him after Uncle Marty instead.

They made their way through some buildings to a scabby back door, where Olly had to edge past a growling collie while Uncle Marty cheerfully called back to him, "It's all right, he's got no teeth."

There seemed to be a lot of Sharpes of all ages inside the house, and none of them took much notice of Olly. The room was dark and seemed crowded with people and furniture. An older man and woman jabbered away to Uncle Marty. Olly found their accent quite hard to understand. The collie had followed them in and spent most of its time with its nose stuck up Olly's bottom. Olly found this embarrassing and annoying but he didn't know what to do about it. He wanted to hit the dog's nose but he wasn't sure whether to believe what Uncle Marty had said about the teeth. Two of the Sharpes stared at Olly with faces that had no expression. They didn't seem to notice what the dog was doing.

Uncle Marty and the older man were still speaking as they made their way outside again. A straggle of Sharpes came with them some of the way. The men seemed to have finished whatever haggling they had been doing and were talking about the hay shed. Mr Sharpe was worried that the roof might blow off and the good hay would get ruined, but Uncle Marty was telling him he was worrying too much and they'd "always managed up to now".

Just then a girl of about Olly's age – presumably one of the Sharpe brigade – came up to Olly and said, "Is that your dad?"

Olly shook his head. The girl looked friendly, but Olly thought – and it was definitely not the kind of thing he usually noticed – that her face, and her clothes, could have done with a good wash. "He's my uncle," he said.

"Do you think he can help us?" she said.

"What with?" Olly asked.

"We can't pay the rent," she said, "so we'll

not be able to go on living here."

"Why do you want to?" Olly asked.

The girl stopped suddenly and turned away. Olly realized he had said something very stupid. He hadn't meant to: it was just that he couldn't think how anyone would want to go on living in this scrappy place, and he forgot that the girl probably didn't want to move because it was her home.

He shrugged. He hadn't meant to offend her. She was probably too stupid to understand anyway.

"Poor old Jim," Uncle Marty said when they got back to the car. "I think the twentieth century's finally caught up with him."

"What do you mean?" Robert asked.

"Just this place," Uncle Marty replied. "It's really, like, No-Hope City. There's too many of them living here. You can't have family farms any more, they're not economical. The Sharpes can't even afford to look after their buildings properly, and pretty soon they're not going to be able to pay their rent any more."

"And what happens then?" said Robert.

"They'll have to leave, won't they?" Uncle Marty said. "They'll have to go and live in some poky little house in Edenbridge or somewhere. They'll have to find jobs or else go on the dole. It'll probably kill them, but what can they do, you know? It's what happens."

"When Aunt Rosie..." Olly began, "I mean,

when they had to move out of Lingerton, long ago, they were all right, weren't they? I mean, they bought Burnside House, and that's a nice house – it's not poky."

Uncle Marty laughed grimly. "There's just one difference: they *owned* Lingerton. The Sharpes don't own Lower Service. They just rent it. The old family that used to live in Miglo Hall – the Hopes – they're the ones who actually own the farm. But no one's seen Mrs Hope for years and years – not since her family all died off. No one even knows if she's alive; but the rent still has to be paid – it's paid to some lawyer in Edenbridge. Maybe Mrs Hope's dead and the lawyers are raking in all the rent money for themselves. Who knows? Who cares?"

"I do," Robert said stoutly. "It's not right. The Sharpes should be allowed to stay here if they want."

"I thought you didn't like the Sharpes," Olly said.

"They should still get to live where they want," Robert replied.

This impressed Olly. He hadn't been able to see past the way there seemed to be so many of the Sharpes, and how dingy their house was, and how they stared, and the funny way they talked and their over-nosey dog. But Robert seemed to have seen the broader picture: he didn't much like the Sharpes either, but he still stuck up for them.

"I think Amanda fancied you a bit," Uncle Marty smiled.

Olly shrugged. "I don't care," he said. But he was starting to feel cross because of his stupid question, and the way Amanda had stopped and turned away.

Uncle Marty started the engine up. Then he nodded to the right, on up the hill. "Look," he said, "I'll just show you where this track goes, right?"

They bumped on up the track, between ridged fields of turnips, and then came to a stop. Over the tops of some trees a battlemented wall had come into view, and Olly realized they must have come by Lower Service farm to the old tower at Scotservice. "I didn't realize this was the same place," he murmured vaguely.

"Oh, we're not going to see old Ronnie, are we?" Robert groaned.

"Just a peep at Miglo Hall," Uncle Marty smiled. "It's a really interesting place." He stopped the car and opened the door. "Come on, it's just a step. Mind the nettles, though. Jim Sharpe could make a fortune if he could crop nettles!"

A path led off towards the trees, and presently they rounded a corner into an ocean of nettles, beyond which they saw Miglo Hall, slouched like a decrepit old grey-green lion

26

in the evening light. "There," Uncle Marty announced, "the one-time home of the vanished Hope family."

The house was long and low, with a pillared entrance not quite in the middle. At one end there was the odd round bit which Olly had glimpsed before, like a dumpy turret.

In this light you could imagine the house had once been grand, though if you looked closely you could make out the streaks of damp and patches of moss-grown decay on the walls. There was no roof – or only the forlorn black sticks of a burned-out roof – apart from on the turret, which still had a cap of mossy slates. Above the pillared entrance something gleamed slightly in the low sun: the remains of what might once have been a glass dome.

"This isn't the way you'd have come last time," Uncle Marty remarked to Olly.

Olly shook his head. "It must have been round the other side. Those trees behind – they must have been the ones where all those crows were."

"Ronnie just doesn't like to be startled," Uncle Marty said. "If we go to the front door, he'll be cool – you'll see."

"You said we weren't going to see him, Dad!" Robert protested. "You said we were just going to have a peep at the house."

"Come on," Uncle Marty coaxed. "It won't hurt to say hello. He's probably watching us right now – he'll be offended if we turn back."

"Well, I'm not going," Robert grumphed. But this time he followed them.

Either old Ronnie had been watching them, or he had some sixth sense which told him when visitors were approaching. He was standing in the pillared porch when they arrived; and his behaviour was very different from when Olly had last seen him.

"Hello there, Marty!" he hollered, with a wide toothless grin. "It's a fine night, isn't it?"

Olly and Robert exchanged a glance which meant: *definitely a couple of slates loose.*

"It is, Ronnie," Uncle Marty agreed. "We were just giving the motor a test run, thought we'd stop by and say hello."

"I like a drive in the motor," Ronnie immediately responded. "It's a nice night for a drive in the motor."

"Oh – sure," Uncle Marty said, surprised. "Sure, why not."

Old Ronnie at once pushed past them and set off the way they had come as though there wasn't a moment to lose. When they reached the car again, he was already sitting in the passenger seat. "Like the cat that got the cream," Robert muttered.

"Where shall we go then?" said Uncle Marty, when they were all in.

"Baldinnie," Ronnie said, as though the answer was quite obvious.

"We can't go to the pub," Uncle Marty told him. "We've got the boys."

Ronnie gave him a pitying look. "We can sit outside. They've got a beer-garden now." He sounded very proud of knowing about something so modern and stylish as a *beer-garden*.

Olly and Robert, sitting in the back of the car with the windows down, couldn't hear much of the conversation between the two men in the front, except on one narrow stretch of the road down a steep hill when Ronnie grabbed Uncle Marty by the shoulder and roared, "Faster, Marty! You're driving too slow!" and Uncle Marty replied, "Behave yourself, Ronnie."

As they were drawing into the carpark of the Baldinnie pub, Ronnie flung his arm out right in front of Uncle Marty's face. "That's my mam's tree!" he roared, pointing in great excitement. "That's where they found my Mam after she went to look for my dad!" He was still pointing and exclaiming as they got out of the car.

Olly saw a large beech tree over behind some new houses, but couldn't see anything special about it. Uncle Marty shook his head patiently. "His mother and her sweetheart – it's some ancient story. He always shouts and roars about it."

Ronnie seemed to forget about his tree suddenly and turned to Robert. "Well, Robert," he said, "you've got your friend tonight; you've got your cousin," though he never actually looked in Olly's direction. Robert grunted, and Ronnie turned and started marching off towards the pub.

"God, is he daft or what?" Olly said as the boys took their seats at one of several empty tables in the shady little beer-garden. "The way he orders your dad about!"

"Everyone orders my dad about," Robert replied. He looked sullen and bored. That was why Olly often didn't like Robert: he never seemed interested in anything.

"That's why he went away," Robert added. "Mum said get out, and he got out."

Neither Robert nor Lucy had spoken about their parents splitting up before, and Olly was quite surprised that Robert had suddenly come out with this now. "He couldn't very well have stayed if she didn't want him to," he said.

"Yes, he could have," Robert growled. "He could have just said he wasn't going. He shouldn't have gone. He's just weak."

Olly said nothing. Robert's outburst was very like some of the things his mother said about Uncle Marty.

Just then old Ronnie appeared again, carefully carrying a large glass of beer with the froth spilling down the sides. He sat down at another table, without paying any attention to the boys, and started drinking greedily.

30

Uncle Marty came out after that, carrying a tray with juice and crisps and a smaller glass of beer for himself. He came over and sat at the boys' table. "We're over here, Ronnie," he called over, but old Ronnie ignored him. "Charming companion." He winked.

Ronnie had almost finished his beer when at last he looked up and noticed them. Then he came over and plonked himself down at their table, knocking everything. "Just about ready for another one, Marty," he said.

Uncle Marty winked again. "I can't afford another one, Ronnie," he said. "These kids are eating me out of house and home."

Old Ronnie looked at Olly for the first time; then gave a strange little start, and frowned and put his glass down suddenly. Olly wondered if that meant he was cross at Uncle Marty's refusing to buy him another drink and was about to start roaring and shouting, but Uncle Marty cut in before he could say anything. "This is Olly," he said. "That's Olive's grandson."

Old Ronnie stared at Olly so hard and for so long that Olly had to turn away. Neither of the others said anything. He tried to pretend he wasn't being stared at, and looked away over the fields across the road as if he had suddenly become very interested in the cows standing around eating grass. He realized slowly that the farm you could see a short distance up the hill beyond the fields was Lingerton. He recognized the big grey shed, but although it wasn't hiding the older farm buildings now, it was impossible to make out anything of them among the shadowy trees.

He heard Ronnie saying, in a strange gruff voice – as if he'd seen a ghost, almost – "That's the angel's face. That's him. That's the angel."

Olly turned to look at him again, though he didn't particularly want to. He half hoped that old Ronnie would be looking at someone else by now, but he wasn't, he was still staring fixedly at Olly, with his mouth hanging open and an expression of utmost wonder in his bleary eyes. Olly glanced appealingly at Uncle Marty.

"What's this, Ronnie?" Uncle Marty said gently. "Olly's no angel, I can tell you. Who are you thinking of?"

"That's the one. I know him," old Ronnie insisted. "My mam spoke to the minister. He told her. The minister says, there's no hims and hers with the angels, there's no boys and girls. You see? They're all the same. The minister told my mam."

There was a long, awkward silence, while Robert and Uncle Marty stared at old Ronnie, and old Ronnie stared at Olly, and Olly went back to staring over at Lingerton farm.

"Well, anyway," Uncle Marty said at length, "we'd best be getting back. These

young lads should be getting to their beds."
Olly and Robert immediately started getting
up, Robert hastily snatching up his half-
finished bag of crisps. There were still a good
couple of hours till bed, but Robert yawned
obligingly. Old Ronnie suddenly remembered
the remainder of his beer and drank it down,
then got up obediently and followed them
back to the car.

They drove back in silence, and when they
had driven as far as they could get, Uncle
Marty got out, went round and opened the
passenger door, practically dragged old
Ronnie out and then went off with him up the
track towards Miglo Hall. The boys stayed
behind.

Robert crunched noisily at his crisps for a
while, then suddenly spluttered and almost
choked. "Angel-Face!" he gasped. "Olly the
Angel-Face!"

"Shut up," Olly said, and threw his own
screwed-up crisp packet at him.

Uncle Marty came back and reported that
he'd persuaded Ronnie to go home. "Sorry
about all that," he added as they started down
the hill again. "Especially you, Olly. It was a
bit weird."

"Was that one of his turns?" Olly asked.

"No," Uncle Marty said. "No, what Ma
calls his turns are just ordinary epileptic fits –
he falls down and goes out for the count for a

33

while. No, this was something else."

"What?" Olly asked anxiously.

Uncle Marty shrugged. "Just one of those things, I guess. Nothing to get your knickers in a twist about. Probably got a bit over excited with the car run and drinking his beer too quickly. Or maybe he wanted to get his own back because I wouldn't buy him any more – thought he'd freak us out instead."

A GLIMPSE
BACKWARDS

"Olly, can I ask you to do something?" Uncle Marty said. "I know you won't be overjoyed at the idea, but it'd be doing me a really big favour."

They were all at the beach, but Olly and Uncle Marty were alone for a little while. Aunt Rosie was off looking for the toilets and Lucy and Robert were bathing and Maudie was testing the effect of her new bikini on a group of boys playing Frisbee.

"What?" Olly said, with a sense of cold foreboding.

"Go and pay a visit to old Ronnie by yourself?"

Somehow, he had already guessed this was what the favour would be. Robert had been calling him "Angel-Face" all day, so it had been very difficult to forget about old Ronnie. He sighed, feeling cornered. "Why?" he asked.

35

"Well, it's like – I told him you would,"
Uncle Marty admitted. "It was the only way I
could get rid of him last night. He wanted to
come back to the car and look at you again."

Olly groaned aloud. "What if he starts
saying crazy stuff?" he whined. "Calling me
an angel and that?"

"Hey," Uncle Marty said, "I can't make you
do it – I wouldn't even try. Look, I can drive
up to Ronnie's tonight and tell him it's not
going to happen. I can take him to the pub and
buy him some more beer. It's cool."

Olly sat up, sighed and looked round.
Everything suddenly seemed very distant,
unreal: blonde sand, blue sea, blue sky, the
restless streaks of surf like mouths full of white
froth opening and closing. For a breathless
moment he felt he was standing at the very
edge of something, knowing he could step
back, yet knowing he would step over...

"I can't make you," Uncle Marty said again,
"but you know, I've got this weird feeling..."

"I know – so have I," Olly breathed, so quietly he hardly heard the words himself.

Just an overgrown hippy. That was what
Olly's mother called Uncle Marty. *A waste of
space.*

"Like, you know, everything's connected,"
Uncle Marty murmured. "Like something's
waiting to happen..."

*   *   *

Olly had forgotten that breathless moment on the beach by the time next morning came, and he felt grudging again. He took Uncle Marty's route, by Lower Service farm, but the track got too rough for cycling just before the farm itself, and was too steep after it, so he had quite a walk. As he approached the farm close, the toothless dog appeared and attached its nose to the back of his heel. When Olly turned to speak to it, it leaped back with a growl and then reattached itself as soon as he turned to go on again. The oldest of the Sharpe boys appeared out of a shed. Olly waved to him, thinking he would call the dog off, but he simply stood and stared without a word until Olly had gone by.

He stood in front of the ruined house. Well, he had made it. What next?

Everything was very quiet. Apart from the occasional muffled *caa!* from the trees behind the house there was no sign of the crows. The meaty scent of sun-warmed nettles filled the air. There was no sign of Ronnie, or of anything.

Olly knew he could turn back and go home again. He had done all he had said he would do. It wasn't his fault if old Ronnie wasn't there.

But instead, he let the heavy old bike gently onto the ground and went forward under the towering stone porch to the front door. He was almost tiptoeing. Now that it came to it, he was curious to see this caravan inside the old ruin. And if old Ronnie wasn't there, all the more reason to have a quick look.

It was a large, roofless space inside, overgrown with nettles, small trees growing here and there against the walls. There was a broad staircase going up at the far end beside a large hole in the wall where more nettles were pressing through, but no windows, only the remains of the glass dome high overhead. It must have been a ballroom or something, back in the olden days.

Ronnie's caravan was over near one of the side walls. It was a large caravan the colour of school custard, pretty ramshackle, green-stained with damp. Why would anyone want to live here? Olly shivered. Only someone really nuts would choose to live in a damp hole like this, even if he did like his privacy.

He had had enough. He turned back to the front door, his trainers scrunching on broken glass in the black earth, matted with nettle roots, which covered the floor.

Then he jumped, because old Ronnie was filling the doorway.

"Do you want to see my hat?" old Ronnie said. "I like Marty, he's my friend. I'll show you my hat."

"If you like," Olly answered with a shrug. Ronnie immediately turned and went back out of the main door into the sunshine. Uncle Marty was right: he was harmless, it was obvious.

"It's over here," old Ronnie said, pointing towards the end of the house and making off in that direction with his clumsy, stumping walk.

They came to a solid, heavy door, with an iron ring instead of a handle. It was ajar, and led straight onto a winding stair up into the strange turret building which seemed to be the only part of Miglo Hall that still had a roof. Old Ronnie went stumping up the stone stairs. Olly followed, and they came to a bare, dusty room, large and circular, with one large window and one large fireplace. It was completely empty apart from the cobwebs which hung in dusty festoons from the ceiling. Ronnie went to the fireplace and turned to Olly with a large grin on his face.

"This is where I keep my hat," he said. "I bet you can't see it."

"No, I can't," Olly agreed. He felt more relaxed now. At least old Ronnie wasn't starting on about angels this time.

"I bet you don't know where it is."

"Up the chimney?" Olly suggested. It didn't look as though there was anywhere else to hide something. Besides, Ronnie was looking very obvious.

Ronnie laughed uproariously. "You're

clever, Olly. Marty's clever too. You're like him. Here's my hat."

Ronnie got himself kneeling down right inside the fireplace and stretched up till his head was out of sight. What he was holding when he appeared again was not a hat but a helmet.

Olly had seen something like it before – or a picture of it. He thought it might have been on a Samurai, or perhaps one of Genghis Khan's warriors. It was open at the front, but had a neck guard at the back and a pointed top. Old Ronnie stroked it fondly. "That's my hat," he crooned. "I wear it. It makes me feel good."

"Right," Olly said. Perhaps this was just old Ronnie's way of making friends, showing off his old helmet.

Obviously it was an old helmet. How did it come to be here? Olly vaguely thought he had heard something about a suit of armour...

"You try it on. Go on," old Ronnie said, grinning hugely, as though he was daring him to do something really exciting.

Why not? It'll keep him happy, Olly thought. Actually the helmet looked oddly put-on-able. There was something which invited you to try it – something smooth and old and substantial. Like Aunt Rosie's bike. "OK," he said.

Ronnie came over to him with the helmet

raised to put on his head. Olly would rather have taken the thing and put it on himself, but he thought he should humour Ronnie. The cool metal slipped over the sides of his head, caressing his cheeks...

There was the faintest flick, like the dip in the lights when you switched a computer monitor on – except that there were no lights in the bare, dusty turret-room. But something had changed, ever so slightly. Without even knowing he was doing it, Olly was gently sliding the helmet up and off his head again – without haste, not as though he had suddenly changed his mind about wearing it; and Ronnie, grinning indulgently, was taking it from him again.

"It's a good hat," Ronnie said heartily. "It makes me feel good."

"It's OK," Olly agreed. "It feels nice."

"You'll come and put my hat on again," Ronnie droned. "You'll come another day, Olly?"

Olly shrugged. "OK."

"You have to go home now," Ronnie told him. No explanation, no sort of politeness. Like a little kid. But Olly had stopped even finding him weird. It was just the way he was. At least you didn't have to try and make conversation, or get embarrassed.

"I'll get my bike," Olly said.

"Bye-bye, Olly," old Ronnie said. "I'm

going to put my hat on again now." He turned away towards the window, and Olly made his way carefully back down the narrow twisting steps, and out into the sunlight of the ordinary morning. Uncle Marty had said he would easily be back by lunch-time. Olly looked at his watch, and saw he should be able to get back in time for the rolls and syrup which Aunt Rosie always served up at half past ten.

Rothes came up to meet him as he swept down the hill. He could make out Burnside House now amongst the jumble of slate-grey and tile-red roofs. The air rushed past, beating in his ears. The scrap of paper from the trees, forgotten since his first visit to Miglo Hall and still trapped in a corner of the wicker basket, *burred* busily in its own private draught. Aunt Rosie's bike was definitely at its best on a steep downhill!

He was suddenly enveloped in a whooshing, diesel-smoky shadow. A large lorry must have been coming down on him without his hearing and decided to overtake him right on the bend. Olly just had time to see a tractor approaching in the opposite direction before his hands took over from his mind and wrenched the handlebars to the left. The front wheel hit the verge and sent him flying gracefully over into the ditch.

His fall was cushioned by a bed of tall

nettles, in which he remained struggling as the lorry swept on down into the village and the tractor roared off up the hill. He thrashed around in the hot whips of the plants, and finally managed to heave himself up onto the verge again, where he lay gasping. There didn't seem to be any part of his body that wasn't stung. He only chose his hand to suck because it seemed to be the most suckable part of himself.

After a little while he swung himself round to a sitting position with his back to the road and gazed down at the Olly-shaped dent among the nettles.

That was when the moment came.

It was the vaguest of images, like a fleeting cloud across the sun, like a momentary dimming of lights. But it was there: a vision of crunching up the gravel path outside Aunt Rosie's kitchen window – golden air – a feeling of huge, long, slow sadness. That was all: the picture in his mind and the feeling; nothing else.

Olly stowed the bike in the garage before limping on up past the loft stairs and round the house. He walked on towards the back door, and glanced up across the hedge towards May Cottage – and then stopped suddenly.

There was something different about May Cottage. It wasn't quite how it ought to look.

He shook his head: too difficult. He could hear
Aunt Rosie and Lucy through the kitchen
window: the buttering and syruping of rolls
must have begun.

He took another step, and stopped again.
That was something else, something about the
way he was walking. What? Another step,
very slowly, putting his foot down carefully...

That was it. The gravel didn't crunch. Aunt
Rosie was always complaining how the paths
had got full of soil so that the weeds always
grew on them, though she actually preferred it
that way, soil and gravel compacted together
into a hard surface, easier for her to walk on
with her bad leg. But what he had remembered, sitting by the side of the road, was
crunching past the kitchen window.

Then, just as he was going in through the
back door, he understood why May Cottage
had looked wrong just now. It was because
there was a hedge in front of it...

But that was how he had always known it:
with a hedge in front of it...

It was like a memory of something. For the
first time, Olly wondered if it had something
to do with having Ronnie's helmet on – that
slight change of the light, as if some minutes
had somehow slipped by...

"Oh, it was a great scandal, when Ronnie
was born," Aunt Rosie was saying. "In those
days you had to get married if you were going

to have a baby, but poor May didn't have anyone. She'd been living with her granny up at the top of the village, but when her granny discovered she was pregnant she turned her out of the house."

"Gosh," Lucy gasped.

"My mother took her in," Aunt Rosie went on. "It was just after we moved here. Well, May had worked for my mother for as long as we could remember, so we all thought it was nice having her back with us again. And now there was a baby as well, so that pleased us a lot."

Uncle Marty was there again in the evening, and wanted to hear about Olly's visit to Miglo Hall. "Well," Olly said, "he wanted to show me his old helmet. That was all, really."

"Helmet?" Uncle Marty said. "What – fireman's? Policeman's?"

"No!" Olly laughed. "It's – you know, metal. Off a suit of armour." Again, something tugged at his memory – something about a suit of armour. But just at that moment something else jumped into his mind and he forgot about the armour. "*Going up to tell her we'd lost something,*" he muttered, frowning.

"What?" Uncle Marty said.

"In the loft," Olly went on, more muttering to himself than speaking to Uncle Marty. "We'd lost something in the loft and we were going up to tell her."

Uncle Marty laughed again. "Hey – just carry on talking, don't mind me."

Olly stared at him absently. Then, finally, grinned. Uncle Marty was all right. A bit of a big kid, maybe. "I think something happened when I put that helmet on," he said at last. "But I've forgotten what."

Uncle Marty got him to describe everything, several times, from the moment old Ronnie approached with the helmet.

"Do you know what it sounds like?" he said eventually. "It sounds like someone else's memory – the gravel still crunched, the hedge hadn't been planted."

Olly agreed. It was like a memory from days long gone. "But whose?" he said.

"I don't know. What did you mean when you said you were going up there to tell *her* you'd lost something? Did you mean May Forester?"

"I don't know," Olly said. "Just – someone. I've got a feeling about who it was, but I can't sort of connect it with anything. Do you remember May when she lived in the Cottage?"

Uncle Marty shook his head. "She died when I was seven."

"So, did you ever lose anything in the loft – something that made you sad?"

"Everyone loses stuff in the loft," Uncle

Marty laughed.

"Anyway, I don't think I was sad because of that."

"What, then?"

"I think it was something about leaving Lingerton."

"Wow – you mean it was a piece of Ma's memory?" Uncle Marty exclaimed. "Is that what... Who did you mean when you said *we*, 'we were going up to tell her'?"

"Like we – were – twins?" Olly gasped. This was getting too weird. Everyday reality seemed to be slipping away.

Uncle Marty stared at him intently. "It's possible, you know? Crunching gravel, no hedge – it could be as much as seventy years ago!"

"Oh man," Olly breathed, clutching his head. "Oh man... How? How is that possible?"

"Who knows?" Uncle Marty said. "Everything's connected. Maybe you're a bit psychic – that's one possibility."

"I don't want to be psychic!" Olly exclaimed. "That's weird stuff."

"Hey, don't worry about it," Uncle Marty soothed. "You know, everything that happens, happens in your head. If you didn't have a brain you wouldn't know there was a world going on. So don't worry if the things that happen in your head seem impossible. When you think about it, the real world's just as impossible."

"I don't buy it," Olly grumbled. "It's bad enough them calling me Angel-Face, without being psychic as well. Tell me another possibility."

"There's an incoming message," Uncle Marty said, looking very serious.

"Where from?" Olly gasped.

"From a UFO, man – from the extraterrestrials." And he looked so solemn it took Olly fully a minute to realize he was joking.

TOO SMALL

Their holiday at Burnside House came to an end. Uncle Marty as usual was to drive Olly and Maudie as far as Kinross, where they would catch their bus home to Glasgow. As they were saying goodbye to Aunt Rosie, Olly glanced in through the open garage door and noticed her old bike propped up against the wall where he had left it. "Goodbye," he whispered; he had grown quite attached to it.

Suddenly he remembered the scrap of paper which had dropped out of the trees. He had noticed it just before his crash with the bike, then forgotten about it again with everything that happened afterwards. Had it survived, or had it been blown away? Aunt Rosie was in the middle of a lecture to Maudie about schoolwork, so he slipped inside and peeped into the basket.

Yes, it was there, still wedged where it had

been in a rough cleft of the wickerwork. Carefully he eased it out. "Look," he said to Uncle Marty outside, "this fell out of the sky."

"Fell out of the sky?" Uncle Marty echoed. Olly had known he would love that idea, that was why he had said it. "What does it say?"

Olly shrugged. "I never looked properly."

Uncle Marty started peering at the faint scrawl. "Wow," he said after a couple of moments. "Hey, this is heavy stuff, man. Listen." Haltingly, and holding the paper up close to his eyes at difficult places, he read out: "*...ec-re-cy unnecessary...* No – *secrecy unnecessary because...* Can't read that. *Ever* – no. *Never be used for evil purposes. I – how so? He – that evil ...* then a smudge *... always liars* – something, something – *conceal things for themselves and keep things secret. But the Living – Book,* I think that is – *requires only honesty. To open yourself ...ead – read,* I suppose, *your life in its lines. A liar cannot...* What is this thing? This is amazing!"

They were all gathered round him by now, except for Aunt Rosie, who hadn't realized what was going on and seemed to be wondering why Maudie wasn't still standing in front of her. "What's on the other side?" Robert said.

Uncle Marty turned the scrap over. "I can't make out much here," he said. "*Combination,* that says."

"Yeah, I got that," said Olly. "Then there's something about despair or something."

"Wait a minute," Uncle Marty said. "Yeah, *exact combination*. Then ...*wer to influence events*. Wow," he said again. "Then down here: *no despairing, no complaining, no giving up, no thought of evil things, no conflict, no battle, no doubt as to...* Hey, this is my kind of thing, man – where did it come from?"

"I thought one of those crows might have been carrying it," Olly told him.

"Right on," Uncle Marty exclaimed. "Yeah, look at the shape of it. This could have been lining a nest, or something, you know?"

"So why was a crow flapping around with it?" Robert wanted to know.

Just then Aunt Rosie reminded them sharply that they would miss their bus if they didn't get a shift on.

"Do you want it?" Uncle Marty said, offering him the scrap of paper back. Olly screwed up his face. "Great, I'll keep it!" He got into the car and carefully put the paper into the glove pocket, then started the engine.

As they left the village, Olly peered out at Service Hill slipping behind them, and thought how strange it was that all the farmland and forest spread around its feet was the Miglo Estate, yet Miglo Hall was a ruin and the people who owned it weren't even around. "What were they like, the people that lived there?" he asked. "Were they rich?"

"The forlorn Hopes? I guess so," Uncle Marty replied. "Henry Hope was supposed to have made his fortune in India. They were more tragic, I think. They were supposed to have been hooked on some big research trip or something, but no one ever found out what. They used to travel a lot. But they all died off apart from Mrs Hope. The son was killed in a crash, Mr H died a year later, the daughter got cancer – the house went on fire – that's how it's a ruin now. Then Mrs Hope disappeared."

"What do you mean, disappeared?" Olly demanded.

"Just that, man. Disappeared. No one saw her again. I can't remember the full story. I just know her lawyers looked after the estate after that, but they all seemed to think she would be back."

"Maybe she went on a cruise," Maudie suggested from the back.

"A long cruise," Uncle Marty said. "Forty years. No, she must be dead by now."

They had been home for three weeks when Maudie set the house on fire.

Olly was coming home one evening, thinking about Lingerton. He quite often did. It was all connected with that feeling of a huge sadness he had got after putting the helmet on. The feeling kept coming back to him at all sorts of times when he wasn't expecting it, and the queer thing was, it felt like his own sadness, not someone else's – as if he was the one who had had to leave Lingerton, long ago. He turned the corner and saw the fire engines.

There was no sign of smoke or fire, but he knew it was Number 29. He thought perhaps Mum had let the chip pan go on fire or something – though two fire engines seemed a bit over the top for that. But as well as the fire engines there were two police cars, one of them with its blue light still flashing, and then he began to get a tight feeling in his stomach.

The house was still there, but there were black marks streaked up the wall from all four windows, and the living-room window was smashed. Disbelieving, Olly thought it seemed no time at all since Mum had been squealing with delight at their new tinted-glass double-glazed units and the newly painted Sunset Pink walls. He saw her there, standing in a huddle with two of the neighbours. She seemed to have a blanket over her shoulders. Dad's car was parked just up the street. There were people everywhere.

Just as he came up, some people started getting out of the back of the police car with the flashing light: a policeman, and Dad, and a policewoman, and Maudie.

Maudie looked very small and forlorn. The grown-ups looked very grim. One of the fire engines started to move away. Various other figures got into the other police car. A small boy, Alistair McCrone, from Number 22 opposite, tugged Olly's arm and said, "Hey, did your sister start that fire?"

Olly shook him off, muttering, "How should I know?" but he could already see it was true. It was just the way everyone looked – as if they were trying to avoid her, as if she was a leper or something. Olly actually felt sorry for Maudie.

"Come on," he heard his father saying. Then he noticed Olly and demanded angrily, "Where have you been, Oliver? Come on, do you want to be left here or what?"

"I was – it wasn't my fault!" Olly managed to stammer. Dad only called him Oliver when he was really angry with him. He felt completely bewildered. Where were they going? Why were they going?

"I don't know what we're going to do." His father's voice again, harsh and threatening. "Nannie's only got the one spare room – and *you'll* be on the floor, my girl."

Olly got into the car. Maudie was sitting hunched in one corner, her arms folded, her head down. She took no notice of him. Neither of them spoke. After a little while their mother got into the front seat. For a while she sat silently staring ahead of her, then suddenly swung round and faced Maudie. "Oh

Maudie," she sobbed, "why did you do it?"

Looking across at Maudie, for a couple of seconds Olly thought that her lip was beginning to quiver. But then she shot a glance at him, looked away again, and her mouth took on its usual cross, determined set. "It was too *small*," she muttered.

"Oh God!" their mother wailed, turning back to face the front again. "What have I done to deserve this?"

Olly stared at Maudie. She was amazing! He almost admired her. But what did she mean? He was too dazed to think straight. He knew he didn't feel angry with her, except that he wanted his supper and felt cross that he would have to wait till they got to Nannie's house over on the other side of Glasgow, but...

In fact, did he understand? After all, they'd always been used to living in the big farm-house with the fields and woods and the burn and all the animals... No, no – that wasn't them, that was the twins, long ago... Yet he couldn't get it out of his head that that was the reason for what Maudie had done. Maybe she'd got used to Burnside House. It was a lot bigger than their own house, with a nice big garden. Maybe that was it...

But they really had been gutted about leaving Lingerton....

He shook his head, to try and straighten his thoughts out. He edged away into his own corner and turned to look out of his window.

Olly and his mother went over to their house on the first Saturday after the fire so that Olly could collect some of his things – in particular an old book about armour his father had found in the Barrows market and Olly had "borrowed". He felt a strange mixture of curiosity and fear as he pushed open the brown-blistered front door, put his foot warily on the sodden hall carpet, and sniffed the damp, acrid air of their transformed home.

The fire had been started in the living-room, and the most severe damage was there. Maudie was lucky not to have killed herself with the poisonous black smoke that had quickly filled the air. ("A pity," their father had commented.) It seemed she had panicked and smashed the window to get out, instead of running through the room to the hall. Smashing the window had let in the air and so the fire had taken in good earnest, but apart from the living-room and the stairs, it was the smoke damage throughout the house which was the worst thing.

Dad had fixed up a ladder because the stairs weren't safe to use, and Olly climbed this while his mother stood in the hall wringing her hands and beseeching him to be careful. The walls looked as though they had been specially painted by a mad artist who would only use black – and what Olly found on his bedroom wall was a masterpiece.

"It's a tree," he breathed, as he squelched in on the soaked carpet. The whole of one wall was taken up with an intricate design of black, like branches – branches and twigs and leaves, forking and twisting, beautiful and horrible.

His and his parents' were the least damaged rooms of the house, except that in the corner by the door of his room the wooden frame inside the wall must have been alight and the smoke had poured out through the tiny crack between the doorpost and the plaster. The top half of the door-frame was charred and eaten away by fire, and the heat had brought the plaster off the rough wooden lath showed through the wall like the insides of a wounded animal. Yellow stains of damp had spread into the wall from the charred wood.

That night, back at Nannie and Granda's, Olly asked if it would be all right to go over to Fife for the October holiday. "Whatever," his father said indifferently. "I just wish we could all go," was his mother's only comment.

"I hope you've got a good story ready for my mother," Uncle Marty said, as they pulled away from the bus stance at Kinross. "She's really hung up on this fire thing, you know? She determined to suss out what's happening in our Maudie's head."

"Well, I don't know!" Olly exclaimed. "I don't know why she did it."

"Not good enough, man," Uncle Marty laughed. "Ma's convinced that you are The Expert on Maudie and she'll give you no peace till she's wrung everything out of you."

Olly groaned and wished he hadn't come.

The journey from Kinross to Rothes took over half an hour, so when they had said all that there was to be said about Maudie, Uncle Marty started telling Olly of the new troubles the Sharpes were having at Lower Service.

"It's been coming for a long time," he said. "They've had a bad year, and it seems they've not been keeping up with their rent. Now the lawyers have got really heavy with them, and say they're going to be put out of the farm if they can't get everything sorted before next summer."

"And can they?" Olly said. Now that he had had a taste of being put out of his home, he felt a good deal more sympathy for the Sharpes. If Amanda Sharpe said to him now, *We won't be able to go on living here any more*, he would answer, *I wish I could help – I really do*. It wouldn't do any good, but at least it would show he understood.

"Get things sorted out?" Uncle Marty said. "Not a chance! Not unless the three older boys go out and get jobs. And they won't – Jim'll just say they're needed about the farm.

"Listen, this is good," he went on. "When the lawyers had been hassling Jim, he went down to the bank to try and get a loan. He said he had a new plan for making money. Do you know what it was? He wanted the bank to give him twenty thousand pounds to buy a team of Clydesdale horses to do the ploughing!"

"Cool," said Olly.

"He said he could have tourists visit the farm and pay to watch them at work!"

"And did the bank give him the money?" Olly asked.

"They fell about laughing! I'm telling you, poor old Jim's going off his trolley, you know?" His smile faded. "I don't know what old Ronnie would do, though. That would be really heavy, if the Sharpes do have to leave. Hey, were you wanting to try that old helmet on again?"

Olly didn't tell Uncle Marty that was his main idea in coming over to Fife. He said, "Do you think old Ronnie'll let me?"

"Let you? It's all he talks about!" Uncle Marty laughed. "I'm really glad you're here; perhaps he'll shut up about it."

"Have you seen the helmet now?" Olly wanted to know.

"Sure."

They were passing the farm road to Lower Service as he spoke, and Uncle Marty suddenly slammed on his brakes. They didn't work very well, so it wasn't exactly an emergency halt. "Do you fancy dropping in on him before we go on to Burnside House?"

Olly shrugged. "If you like."

Soon they were bumping up the rough track, and Olly began to wonder what was really going on. It was one thing, old Ronnie insisting that he come and try on the helmet. But now Uncle Marty had got involved – and couldn't even wait to get to Burnside House before he was suggesting that they went off to see the thing.

"Why do you think he wants to see me so much?" Olly asked, as the squat dark shape of Scotservice Tower came into view above the autumn-coloured trees.

"I don't know," Uncle Marty said. "But I think there's something going on."

Exactly. But that didn't really explain anything. "What kind of thing?"

"Who knows, man? But, you know – everything's connected."

The last time they had heard Uncle Marty saying that, he and Maudie and Lucy and Robert had fallen about laughing. It was such a totally Uncle Marty thing to say. Now Olly didn't feel like laughing about much at all.

POSSESSED

"Did he let you try the helmet on?" Olly suddenly asked.

"Sorry, man," Uncle Marty grinned. "You are the chosen one – *Angel -Face, wearer of the helmet of ancient times.* It is ancient, by the way. I think it's Scythian. I looked it up in some books."

"What's Scythian?" Olly asked. He had not found his father's book much help.

"It's more who than what," Uncle Marty told him. "The Scythians were this bunch of nomads. About two, three thousand years ago. I think it was them that first tamed horses or something."

"Cool," Olly said.

Miglo Hall in autumn looked shabby and depressing, and when old Ronnie appeared in the huge porchway, he matched his surroundings. But his face was beaming. "Hello, Olly,"

61

he roared, completely ignoring Uncle Marty. "Do you want to put my hat on again? Come on!" He would have led them straight off if Uncle Marty hadn't stopped him.

"Hey, hang on, Ronnie," Uncle Marty said. "Olly's just had a long bus journey. Do you not think a cup of tea and a biscuit would be nice, maybe?"

"Biscuits?" old Ronnie echoed. "I've got biscuits."

"I know you have," Uncle Marty said, "I brought you them yesterday."

"I've got good biscuits," Ronnie agreed. "I've got four left." He disappeared inside.

"Only four – you guts!" Uncle Marty said. "He probably doesn't eat properly," he added in a lower voice as they followed him, "but what can you do? He likes his independence. The Sharpes give him eggs and potatoes and stuff, but the worry's always whether he will manage to get them cooked without setting the place on fire – oops, bad subject, sorry."

The inside of the caravan was dark and damp and didn't smell very nice. It was exceedingly untidy, and Uncle Marty and Olly sat on filthy old ripped cushions while Ronnie fussed around a gas stove and produced three chipped mugs and a square tin box with four chocolate biscuits inside a border of rust. Olly didn't much like the look of them, but he thought he ought to have one to be polite. As he was eating it, old Ronnie suddenly announced, "That's my dad, do you know my dad?"

Olly looked round, bewildered. He seemed to remember that no one had known old Ronnie's dad. Ronnie was gazing at a kind of battered chest of drawers next to Olly, which was covered with all kinds of rubbish, and Olly eventually made out an old photograph that was propped at the front of it.

"Look!" Ronnie exclaimed, leaning over and grabbing the photo and thrusting it at Olly. "That's him, he's marked."

It was a faded photograph that showed a group of soldiers in uniforms. One of them had an egg-shaped border drawn round him in very faint pencil. This was quite a young man, holding a gun upright against his arm with a very serious expression on his face. Olly turned the picture over. There was some handwriting on the back, neat and large but very faded: *Here I am with the platoon. From your ever-true – Ronald.* Next to that there was a number, scrawled untidily in pencil: a phone number, it looked like.

"Do you like my dad?" Ronnie demanded, then, without waiting for a reply, "I do. I like him fine. Do you want to put on my hat now? My hat's good. I talk to my mam, and I talk to my Auntie Betty."

Olly hadn't finished more than half of

his tea, but he was quite glad to get out of the dingy caravan with its awful stale smell. This time Uncle Marty made no objection to going.

As old Ronnie blundered ahead of them up the narrow stair into the turret-room, Olly muttered to Uncle Marty, "What's the point of this? We don't even know that it was the helmet that made me have that dream-thing last time."

"You heard the man." Uncle Marty smiled. "He talks to his mam and he talks to his Auntie Betty. If he can, so can you."

"I haven't got an Auntie Betty and I came here to get away from my mum," Olly muttered.

"Hey, hang loose," Uncle Marty said. "We're going to be scientific."

Ronnie had already fished the helmet out from its hiding-place and was bearing it over towards them.

"Hold it there, Ronnie," Uncle Marty said, holding up his hand. "Let's not rush. You know, you're used to this old thing and it makes you feel good, that's cool. But you've got to let Olly get a bit used to it too, OK?"

"OK, Marty." Ronnie grinned agreeably, and continued to advance on Olly.

Uncle Marty tried again. "Ronnie, can I just see the hat a moment? There's a couple of things I'd like to show Olly."

"What is it, Marty?" he asked. "What do you want to show Olly?"

He let Uncle Marty take the thing from his hands and hold it up, turning it slowly so that the light moved, sheening its brownish surface. "See, Olly," Uncle Marty said. "It's made of bronze. The pointed bit on the top's copper. I think it's from the suit of armour Ma and Olive used to play with, long ago, over at Scot-service. I wonder how it got here? Ronnie won't tell me, will you, Ronnie?"

"That's right, Marty." Ronnie grinned, but it was hard to tell if he had even been listening.

"OK, Ronnie," said Uncle Marty. He was speaking softly and slowly, as if trying to keep everyone calm. "Why don't you let Olly hold the helmet as you're putting it on his head..."

"All right, Marty," Ronnie said again, though he didn't seem to have much idea what Uncle Marty was talking about.

He took the helmet and held it over Olly as he had done before. "OK, Olly," Uncle Marty said, "just slowly and carefully. Let your mind go blank. Just try and concentrate on what you're doing – what kind of reactions you have."

Olly reached up and touched the helmet. It felt cool as they slipped it down over his head. He had not noticed the last time what a good fit it seemed to be – almost as though it had been made for someone his age.

"All right?" he heard Uncle Marty say.

"Yes, I'm all right," Olly returned, and stood, feeling the helmet. He noticed it seemed both lighter and heavier than it looked. Apart from that, there was nothing.

This was a stupid situation. He was just an ordinary boy standing in a deserted room in a ruined house, wearing a helmet that might or might not have been thousands of years old, being stared at by two adults who both, in their own ways, weren't quite right in the head. Why had he let this happen? "I don't know what it's supposed to do now," he said aloud.

"Hasn't it changed anything?" Uncle Marty enquired. He looked disappointed.

Olly shook his head, frowned and shrugged.

Uncle Marty half turned away. "Can't have been the helmet after all, I suppose," he muttered. "Must have been that lorry knocking you off the road."

"Can I take it off now?" Olly said.

"Whatever," Uncle Marty smiled. "You do look a bit stupid – standing there with your mouth open and a tin pot on your head."

Olly grinned. Perhaps Uncle Marty was all right. Perhaps he'd done all this to humour old Ronnie again. But why? He could ignore old Ronnie, surely – not visit him – pretend he didn't exist?

There's no one else can do it.

That was odd. He had just heard those words echoing in his ears. And it was his mother's voice which had spoken them. And that, Olly knew, was impossible. Yet there it was; he could imagine the way her face looked as she spoke, almost smell the smell of breakfast toast – almost feel the solid pine table where he was sitting, looking over to where she knelt with her back to him, holding the bread against the hot coals with her toasting-fork...

Wait a minute. He shook his head, because the picture in his memory was becoming too solid and it was making him uncomfortable. It wasn't just Mum's voice – it was the toast. They had a toaster at home, a perfectly good electric toaster. Mum had never made toast at a fire with a toasting-fork!

It was time to get this thing off. It obviously did mess with your mind. He pushed at it, hard at first, then more gently as he felt it jamming. It was more difficult to get off than it should be – as though it was being held on his head by suction.

Your piece of toast.

What was that! Olly nearly jumped, stumbled, swung round, finished up staring wildly at the wall behind him. Nothing there. No one. That hadn't been the echo, the memory of a voice: that was the real thing!

"What is it, Olly?" he heard Uncle Marty saying.

"My piece of toast," Olly mumbled. He could see it for a moment, the scorched edges of the bread, the purple jam... He remembered about the helmet and pushed up at it again. Why was it taking so long to come off?

"What?" Uncle Marty said.

"That's my mam!" Ronnie loudly exclaimed, laughing his empty-headed laugh.

The helmet felt like a vice on his skull. Tug, tug.

That's your last bit. You'll be late. The maister's taking you today.

The words were as clear as anything. It wasn't his mother's voice at all – he must have been mixed up before. Why wouldn't this thing come off? He heaved and grunted, red-faced with effort.

"'Smy turn now, Olly," Ronnie's voice came, good-natured but insistent.

The helmet came off, almost with a pop, and to his utter astonishment Olly found he was roaring with laughter! He was laughing so much there were tears on his cheeks. He dropped the helmet on the floor and doubled up with his hands on his knees, gasping for breath. He saw Uncle Marty down on his hands and knees, scrabbling for the helmet and at the same time looking up anxiously into his face. That made him laugh all the more.

"What is it, Olly? What is it? What is it?" he kept saying.

"The coffee bun!" Olly gasped, and was seized by another fit of hysterics. It was frightening – he knew it was frightening because this wasn't the way he laughed, this wasn't him laughing – and yet it was so funny. Old Ronnie was roaring with laughter too. He was holding the helmet now, and turning it round as though preparing to put it on his head. Uncle Marty, still on his hands and knees, stared up at them both in stupefaction.

Olly gulped. "I want to go now," he said abruptly, and turned towards the stairs. Old Ronnie took no notice of him.

As soon as Olly got outside he went marching quickly off back to the car, never looking round. He knew that something very strange had happened and he didn't like it at all; he had an idea that if he walked like this – quickly and regularly, concentrating only on walking – it would somehow be better. Like a soldier marching, swinging his arms, one-two, one-two.

Uncle Marty caught up with him. He seemed to have been running. "Olly – Olly," he panted, catching him by the shoulder, "are you all right, man? What happened?"

"Nothing, I'm all right," Olly replied, giving his shoulder a slight shake and continuing on his way, one-two.

They got into the car in silence. The silence continued until they were practically into Rothes.

"I don't want to do that again," Olly announced flatly. "I wish I hadn't come. I don't ever want to go there again."

"OK," said Uncle Marty.

As they drove through the village, Olly suddenly asked, "What's it like being possessed?"

Uncle Marty shrugged. "Pass. Like someone else has taken over your mind?"

Olly was silent for a little. They slowed down, preparing to turn in through Aunt Rosie's gate. "No," he said eventually. "No, it felt like me. I think. Except I don't really know where 'me' stops and something else starts. What's a coffee bun?" he asked.

"Pass," Uncle Marty said again. "A bun you have with your coffee? I heard you saying that – you don't know why?"

Olly shook his head. "But I think I knew at the time," he said. "I might have known if I hadn't … if I hadn't come back."

"Come back?" Uncle Marty echoed. "Were you away somewhere?"

Olly said nothing, but started to get out of the car. He felt shaky, but he was beginning to recover. He hoped Aunt Rosie would have made some of her thick potato soup.

OPENING THE BOOK

An hour later, stuffed with as much thick potato soup as he could hold – to say nothing of the bread and strawberry jam and sponge cake – Olly began to wonder what he would be doing over here at Aunt Rosie's on his own if he didn't go to see old Ronnie again. He had already had a good grilling from Aunt Rosie about Maudie and her wickedness, and he knew there would be more. Uncle Marty said that Lucy would be coming over in a couple of days, but Robert wouldn't, this time. He also said that if Olly was short of something to do he could have a look through the old books in the loft, and see if there were any not too badly mouldered that they could sell.

Would it really be that awful going back up to old Ronnie's again and trying to find out more about the strange helmet?

"Have you any idea what a coffee bun is,

Ma?" he heard Uncle Marty asking.

Olly looked up, startled.

"A coffee bun?" Aunt Rosie repeated, smiling, with a look as of some ancient recognition. "Well, I must have done once, though I can't remember now. But there was an awful funny thing happened about the coffee bun. Oh, ages ago."

You could tell by her voice that this meant the Lingerton days, when they had the pony trap that was pulled by little Polka; the twins would be run to school in it in the mornings by the maid, May Forester. But on one particular morning May refused to take them; she had too much to do in the kitchen – something to do with sloes, the maister's sloes... Who was the maister, and what were his sloes?

"Well, my father was absolutely furious," Aunt Rosie was saying. Olly shook himself. Had she been telling the story all this time? He wasn't sure how much she had said and how much was in his mind, like a memory – a picture, small and clear, of a large, gloomy kitchen with a huge pale table in the middle, whitewashed walls, a fire burning behind the black bars of a grate... Aunt Rosie's father was the maister – though in the kitchen May was queen, and not even the maister would be allowed in.

"Things were different in those days," Aunt Rosie said. "I think my father thought it was

a bit beneath his dignity to be seen in public
with the children. But I remember my mother
saying to him, 'Well, you dig the garden for
me, and I'll take them' – but she was only teas-
ing him, because digging the garden was
woman's work. So my father just had to get
Polka and the trap…"

Yes, May was cross this morning – hot and
bothered and very cross. "Your piece of
toast." It was slapped onto the table, not even
on a plate. It was something to do with the fire
not heating up properly when she had all that
water to bring to the boil. "As if I hadna
enough on my hands wi'oot him and his
blooming plooms…"

Olly could hear her, see it, and at the same
time hear Aunt Rosie's singsong voice in the
other, only slightly more modern, kitchen of
Burnside House. He could see her, and Uncle
Marty – and his own hands on the table in
front of him, his fingers picking up cake
crumbs from his plate – and at the same time
Daddy's knee in its brown-checked tweed, the
dipping reins, Polka's dark brown rump, the
backs of her ears, the blinkers she had to wear
because she was *such* a fidget… It was as
though his vision was split in two, and the
images were small, feverish, yet so sharp and
clear.

Daddy was muttering about how slow
Polka was. He thought she was far too fat and

73

it was all May's fault for spoiling her. But however much he flicked the whip and made impatient clicking sounds through his teeth, Polka kept up the same steady pace, ears alert, head shifting from side to side as much as the bit would allow her – she always liked to look at the view! So they sat, watching and listening – the clopping of the hoofs, the creaking of wood and leather, the jingling harness, the quiet rumble of the wheels – steadily up the long hill from Baldinnie, and then winding down the long hill towards Edenbridge. The leaves on the trees were golden, and brown leaves scuttered earthwards in a smurr of rain on the chilly east wind; but they had their leather button-boots and their warm coats on and the cold didn't reach them.

So they came round the corner and among the grand stone houses on the outskirts of the town, joining the road from Newport that ran through the middle of the Municipal Park towards the Cross. Ahead stood the first buildings of the town centre, the Regency Hotel on the right, which always gave you a little shiver because everyone knew it was haunted, and – oh dear! – the baker's shop on the left. *Does Daddy know about Polka and the baker's?* He was bound not to, because he'd be bound to disapprove. Daddy lifted his hat and gave a small bow to a man and a lady walking along the pavement; he was very much on his dignity this morning. *Oh, Polka, don't...*

Polka stopped. They were right outside the baker's shop, whose door was standing open. As always, there was a wonderful smell coming from it.

"Walk on, lass," Daddy said. He was still calm, but you could see a slight flush beginning on his cheeks, spreading out from his whiskers. Then, "Walk on!" again, with rising impatience, raising the whip and shaking the reins.

Polka was immovable.

"She always gets a coffee bun," Olly whispered.

"Nonsense," Daddy snorted. "I've never heard the like. Come on, walk on." The whip flicked.

Then Polka did move – but not in the right direction! Horrified, delighted, they watched...

"Well, Polka always had her coffee bun," Aunt Rosie said, "and she just thought, if the girl wouldn't bring it out for her she'd have to go and get it herself, and that's what she did: she went right up the steps and put her head in through the door of the shop! Well, my father was mortified. There was a terrible row when he got back home. He said he would never be able to show his face in Edenbridge again..."

Uncle Marty was laughing, and Olly found he was too, but this time it was his own laughter, not that helpless laughter when you thought your insides were going to fall out or you could pee yourself. He had never thought about it before, but it suddenly seemed obvious to him that girls laughed differently from boys.

And that was how he had been laughing, in the deserted turret-room of Miglo Hall – the way girls laugh. The thought made him move uncomfortably on his chair, and his laughter stopped.

Later, in the quiet of his bedroom, the strangeness of everything hit him again. Aunt Rosie might seem like a very normal person – or as normal as you could expect a really old person to be – but his mind was getting filled with bits of her memories, and that didn't seem at all normal. That was freaky.

Yet it was only the thought of it that was freaky; the actual thing, the actual memories, were all right. They were homely, nice.

Then another thought struck him, even freakier. Perhaps the memories he was getting weren't Aunt Rosie's at all; they could just as well be the memories of the other one – they were twins, after all, absolutely identical – Grandmother Olive, who had died forty years ago. Olly had been *inside* the story of Polka and the coffee bun: he had been right there, one of the girls, one of the twins. The stern tall man with the bushy whiskers hadn't been

Great-Grandfather Martin MacClay of Lingerton – he had been "Daddy"!

So which of the twins had Olly been? *No* – he had to not think about that. That was too much.

He didn't get a chance to speak to Uncle Marty alone until the next day. "What was wrong with you last night?" Uncle Marty wanted to know. "You really spooked me. You looked as though you were seeing things."

"I was," Olly told him. He described what had happened to him as Aunt Rosie had been speaking.

"So," Uncle Marty said thoughtfully, "it was the same memory – the same as you'd had earlier, with the helmet on."

"Yeah, it was like we were filling the missing bits in. Aunt Rosie was talking, and I was seeing all this stuff – I mean, like, I was really there, I was in two places at once." He felt fairly calm and matter-of-fact now, but he still had to make an effort not to think too hard about it, just in case it got freaky again.

"When you think about it," Uncle Marty said, "before Ronnie got it, who were the last ones to put that helmet on? It could have been my mother and my Auntie Olive. You know? It's like some memories kind of got rubbed off inside the helmet…"

He was silent for a while, then went on,

"I've got this weird feeling; it's like there's something – something from really far away – trying to focus in on us. Like there's a message trying to get through to us. Don't you feel that?"

"No," Olly said.

"Weird, too, old Ronnie calling you an angel. Angel – it just means *messenger*, you know? That's its real meaning. Like, this something's using you, and the helmet, and these old memories, to get something else across... A message. You know?" He gazed appealingly at Olly.

"I don't know," Olly said. "Maybe. I don't know – I don't want you to freak me out. Yes, OK. Maybe there's a message. But what sort of message? What's it saying?"

"It's hard to say, you know? If it was like – a ghost? A ghost that comes to tell you about a secret will, or buried treasure... I don't believe that stuff though. But, what if it was just...? What if ghosts... I mean, who says that ghosts have to be the ghost of *someone*? You know?"

"What else can a ghost be?"

"I don't know, man," Uncle Marty said, scratching his head. "Suppose it's like – something that floats about in people's memories, you know, like a fish floats about in water. No, not a fish, like a current of water – you know, a thing that kind of *stretches* through time... Yeah, a time ghost..."

"A time ghost," Olly repeated. "I don't know what that is."

"Me neither." Uncle Marty grinned. "Pay no attention. I'm babbling. I don't know what the hell's going on. But, could you see your way to trying the helmet on again?"

"Maybe," Olly muttered. "But, you know, Ronnie, he puts me off. I don't mind him, but it's hard to concentrate."

"I know what you mean," Uncle Marty said. "It's difficult. You might be able to nip up on the off-chance – you never know when he might be away. Hey, maybe if it's meant to be, it'll be. You could just mosey on up some time and see what happens."

For the moment, there didn't seem too much chance of moseying anywhere, because Aunt Rosie decided to put Olly to work. The next morning he was given the job of hacking down a large laurel bush in the next-door neighbour's garden which had grown too big and was covering one of the windows in Aunt Rosie's garage. In the afternoon he was sent to the loft to sort out the books.

He poked about in the bookshelf. He was still feeling a bit tired after his morning's hacking. Everything had a film of slightly damp dust on it. The black shelves were peppered with woodworm holes. The books had small blue flowers of mould on them, and spiders had built spider-cities in every available space.

Aunt Rosie came clumping up the stairs. She watched him for a while, then waved her stick towards the bottom shelf. "Just be careful at the bit behind," she warned him. "There's a place where books were always slipping down and disappearing into the wall."

Olly pulled books out and looked at them vaguely. But his mind wasn't really on it. *Whose* memories had he been having? Was there a way to stop thinking *we* and to think instead *me and Olive*, or *me and Rosemary*? But there seemed no way – unless he could manage to control the memories better. Without old Ronnie there...

Lucy arrived, and that gave Olly the chance of slipping off by himself.

He didn't take the most direct route, by Lower Service. He didn't want any Sharpes staring at him. He left the bike in the National Trust carpark and walked through the woods. That way he could avoid old Ronnie too.

He stepped over the trampled-down fence. A stubble of crackling brown sticks was all that was left of the willowherb.

Even though he had been expecting it, Olly jumped with the explosion of harsh sound from the crows at the first crackle. Dark clouds lifted from the golden treetops, filling the air with fantastic black shapes. He gazed upwards. They were all around, circling him, and their din became strange – distant and metallic, yet all the more oppressive for that. Were they drawing their circle in on him? He believed they were – coming lower, nearer, tighter...

This wasn't a good place to be alone in. Forget concentrating with the helmet. He wanted someone else with him. He crept along the front of Miglo Hall as the crows circled and swirled, past the closed door of the turret, along to the shelter of the huge pillared porch, and into the ruined hallway.

The noise seemed less here, even though there was no roof. Olly stood, relieved, poised to go on to the door of the caravan.

The sound faded and it became very quiet. He had been letting his imagination get on top of him. There was no sign of Ronnie. Perhaps, by some luck, he had arrived here on one of the few occasions when he wasn't around. *Maybe if it's meant to be, it'll be.* He should stick to what he had decided. Hesitantly, he turned from the caravan again. A blackbird sounded its warning trill and swooped off out of one of the bushes through the gap in the far wall. The silence closed around him again.

Then, through one of the open doorways leading out of the hallway, he saw someone. An old woman, tall and thin and straight,

81

wearing a soft pink jersey and a necklace of pearls. He took in the details all at once. She was standing just through the doorway, gazing out of the window.

Of course, the idea *ghost* crossed Olly's mind, but not in a way that frightened him, even though his skin felt electric. It was simply the feeling: *so this is what it's like to see a ghost*. Soundlessly, he crept towards her.

She didn't look round or pay him any attention. And just as he reached the doorway she turned and left the window. Olly watched her move across the room. About halfway across she stopped, and raised one hand. Then, standing so, with her hand raised, she faded – disappeared.

That was too much. Olly broke and ran for it, vaulted through the window into the blustery grey of an ordinary autumn day. Then he ran heedless, never stopping till he had reached the carpark and stood, gasping and wheezing, over Aunt Rosie's bike.

THE MESSAGE

He gritted his teeth and cycled. It was better on the up-slopes, because there you just had to get your head down and crank-crank-crank on the creaking pedals. At the road junction he turned left, not right: towards Edenbridge, not Rothes. *Just please let Uncle Marty be there.*

Edenbridge was packed with cars and people, but he scarcely noticed, and headed for Uncle Marty's flat by the quickest route he knew. He didn't look at any of his surroundings until he had to stop at a pedestrian crossing.

Then, on a wall, he saw a plate with the words *Regency Mews, Flats 5-8*, and for the first time he started to tie together his images of Edenbridge in the past and Edenbridge now. That chilly autumn morning, as they drove into Edenbridge in the trap, they had seen the Regency Hotel. It was flats now. So across the road must be where the old baker's shop was, where Polka had climbed the steps. There was, no shop there now, just some large ground-floor windows with glass that you couldn't see through. On the glass, in gold letters, he read: *Crooke, Barbour and Savidge, Solicitors and Notaries.* It was part of a lawyers' office. One of those windows must be where the old door had stood open to let out its glorious warm smell.

Olly sat on at the crossing, even after the lights had changed. He wondered if these were the lawyers who were going to put the Sharpes off their farm if they didn't pay their rent. Straight ahead of him was the War Memorial on the edge of the town park. He remembered now, it hadn't been there, that long-ago morning. The park had looked a lot rougher – more like a field – and there had been no War Memorial.

It was strange, he had never thought about the War Memorial not being there. It was a huge block of polished pink stone with a great grey angel standing on top with its wings half spread. Its head and shoulders were iced with pigeon droppings. From this distance the names of all the dead soldiers looked like little stacks of black lines, whole lines and broken lines...

A couple of girls were crossing the road in front of him, staring at his bike and

84

sniggering. He flushed and pushed off, going through the lights on the red, picking up speed as he rounded the end of the park and then riding off like mad up the quiet street that led to Uncle Marty's flat.

Uncle Marty was there, just going in through the door as Olly came careering up and staggered off his bike. "Hey, peace, man!" he exclaimed, holding his palm up. "Are you OK?"

"No," Olly hissed. "No, I'm not. There was something. I was up there, and I saw something – a ghost. I saw a ghost…"

"Come on," Uncle Marty said, turning back to the door. Olly already felt better: in fact, he didn't think he had ever felt quite so glad to see Uncle Marty before.

It wasn't a very nice flat. You could see that even before you went in the door, which badly needed a coat of paint. You could barely read the name label – *Martin Gellatly* – which was curled up at one end as if trying to escape from the doorbell. Inside, piles of papers and books were scattered everywhere amongst bits of broken furniture that Uncle Marty was supposed to be repairing. His strange little electric cooker-cum-oven, which he always complained about because it didn't make toast, sat greasily on a table with various dirty plates and knives littered around it. Lucy was always going on at her father to keep his flat tidier, but Uncle Marty would say, "I don't know, kiddo, you know – a tidy room is the sign of an empty mind." That would make Lucy furious, because she was very neat.

Olly threw himself down in one of the armchairs and buried his face in his hands. "I think I want this to stop," he moaned. He explained everything that had happened.

"Well," Uncle Marty said, "either the helmet has affected you even when you're not wearing it, or else you really are psychic."

"Maybe there was just a ghost there," Olly growled. "You don't have to be psychic to see a ghost."

"I don't know anything about ghosts, man," Uncle Marty said. "You know? Just because you see someone disappear it doesn't mean they're a ghost. There's teleportation, astral projection, you know – maybe it was someone from a parallel dimension—"

"Was it Mrs Hope, Uncle Marty?"

Olly surprised himself with this suggestion more than he did Uncle Marty, who just went on doing what he had been doing before – which was tickling his nose with the end of his ponytail.

"You know," Uncle Marty said, and sneezed, "that's a very savant suggestion. And you know what I'm thinking? That room that goes off the main hall up at Miglo – that was probably the library, and you know what that means?"

Immediately he said it, it hit Olly. He had recognized the movement the old lady had made, it was just that he hadn't been able to connect it to anything. But it was really obvious, when you thought "library". "She was putting a book up on a shelf," he said.

"Hey, you're almost as quick as me!" Uncle Marty exclaimed. "Now, what book?"

That stumped Olly. "What do you mean, what book?" he exclaimed. "How should I know what books she had in her library?"

"Hey, everything's connected," Uncle Marty murmured. He went over to the debris-littered table, moved a few things about, and picked something up – a scrap of paper, tattered, brown-edged...

"Oh no, come on," Olly said. "How do you know that? That thing just dropped down from the trees."

"Right in front of your feet," Uncle Marty reminded him. "Not fifty yards away, not an hour before: right at your feet just as you came walking along. I'm telling you, kiddo, it's not coincidence: it's this *message*."

"Yeah, but what message? Who from? Like, you said that thing about a time ghost, but—"

"Forget the time ghost, man," Uncle Marty said. "I don't even know what that is. But about the message – maybe it's simpler than you think, you know? Suppose it's like it says on this bit of paper: a message about a *Living Book*."

"I can't remember what it said," Olly grumbled. He knew it was strange, the way the bit of paper had fallen down to him, but he couldn't really accept that some crow had dropped a message specially for him. "Anyway, what's a *Living Book*?"

"Dunno. But it says stuff about it, whatever it is; it says you have to be honest, and you have to read your life in its lines and – just stuff like that."

"So is that what that wifie was putting on the shelf?" Olly asked.

"Search me, man. This bit of paper may be all that's left of the book that you saw her putting on the shelf. Maybe *it* was this Living Book, or maybe it was just a book *about* this Living Book. Maybe the message is that we have to look for this Living Book..."

"It's not a very clear message, is it, Uncle Marty?"

"I know," Uncle Marty admitted. "But you'll see. If it is a message, then I bet you something more'll come up. Soon."

Olly was silent. There didn't seem a great deal he could say.

"Anyway," Uncle Marty went on, "would you like to know where I've just been? You remember that picture? The photo in old Ronnie's caravan?"

"Ronnie's dad? Sure."

"I was checking it out, down at the British Legion," Uncle Marty said. "I found a copy of the very same photo – same unit, same place, everything – the names of all the men. His was *Ronald Ewart*... Well, I might have heard the name before, I don't remember. That's not the main thing though. I found this list. Ronald Ewart was killed at Amiens in 1918, the last year of the war."

"Right," said Olly, mystified. "So?"

"Well," Uncle Marty said slowly. "Ronnie was born in 1924."

Olly had to think about this a little. The dates of all these long-ago years got squashed up together somehow, and 1924 seemed just round the corner from 1918. But it wasn't really. 1924 was six years after 1918. Six years: half his own lifetime. "So – that soldier couldn't have been Ronnie's dad," he said at length.

"So why does Ronnie think he is?" Uncle Marty asked.

"Well, he's daft, isn't he?" Olly said. "He's like – in a world of his own, right?"

"He's not as daft as you think," Uncle Marty said thoughtfully. "I sometimes think old Ronnie knows a lot more than he lets on."

"Like – about angels?" Olly grinned.

Uncle Marty came over to collect Lucy that

evening, and over supper he brought the conversation round to Mrs Hope again.

Aunt Rosie wasn't too helpful. "I didn't see very much of Mrs Hope," she said. "I was away at university by the time my mother got friendly with her. My mother would visit Elspeth Hope – that was the daughter – when Elspeth was dying of cancer. I think Mrs Hope felt grateful to her for that; after Elspeth died she gave my mother that hallstand by the front door. It's the only really valuable piece of furniture I've got."

They all trooped down the hall to look at this piece of furniture. It wasn't really a hallstand at all, it was just that Aunt Rosie didn't know what else to call it. It was a shiny, red-painted thing in all sorts of wonderful shapes – bearded faces and dragons and snarling heads. It was Chinese, she informed them.

"There's something in there," she said, prodding with her stick at the handle of a small drawer. "I don't know where it came from."

Uncle Marty tugged at the drawer and fished out a small picture frame with what looked like a text in it. "I remember this, Ma!" he exclaimed. "I haven't seen it for years. Was it in here all the time?"

But Aunt Rosie had gone stumping off up the hallway; she had heard the kettle whistling in the kitchen.

"It's one of those samplers," Uncle Marty

explained. "Girls used to have to do them long ago to show off their needlework. This isn't a real sampler, though, it's more an embroidered text, but there's her name – whoever did it."

Olly looked closely at the frame. The name was across the top in blue lettering: *Elisabeth de Scyras, 1879.* There were also some tiny words in green lettering down each side, but the text itself was in large red letters. The background colour was like an old dish-cloth. He read out:

Forlorn, with no belonging,
Where is the Beloved?
Still you press on.
You join yourself to those who can help.
You come, imperfectly,
You are half-seen,
You are in confusion.
Your day comes; your page can be read:
You laugh for joy –

"What's all that about?" he demanded.

"It's beautiful," Lucy sighed. "It's a love-poem."

"Is it?" Olly said. "Why do you have to read a page then?"

"It's poetry!" Lucy protested.

"I think that's right, kiddo," Uncle Marty said. "These little words in the margin: it's two German words, repeated over and over: *ganz* and *gebrochen* – 'quite' and 'broken'. Look: *broken, quite, quite broken – broken, broken, broken*; and on this side: *broken, quite, quite, quite broken, quite...* Whoever wrote this was gutted. Suicidal, you know?"

"That's tragic," Lucy whispered. "Who is that – Elisabeth de Scyras?"

Aunt Rosie was coming down the hall again. "We don't know," she said. "My mother always called Mrs Hope Betty, so that's short for Elisabeth – but I don't know if her maiden name was de Scyras. The de Scyras family built Scotservice Tower long ago – 'Service' is supposed to come from 'Scyras'." She ran her fingers gently over the frame before putting it back into the drawer. "I didn't think she'd have been this old, though," she added.

"Old Ronnie said something about a Betty – his Auntie Betty," Olly remembered.

"That's right," Uncle Marty said. "That's a bit weird, isn't it?"

"Ronnie Forester never had an Auntie Betty," Aunt Rosie snorted. "He'd have just been havering. He's not all there, you know."

Olly grabbed Uncle Marty by the arm just as he and Lucy were leaving. "You were right!" he whispered.

"What about?" Uncle Marty whispered back.

"That something else would come up. And now it has."

"What?"

"That text!" Olly hissed. "Don't you see?"

"No. What?"

"*Your page can be read* – doesn't that sound like a book?"

"Oh." Uncle Marty sounded surprised. "I never thought about that. It was just something I remember from when I was young."

In bed that night, thoughts flew round Olly's head like scattering leaves. Everything about the past few peculiar months came and went: the helmet, Aunt Rosie's stories, the incredible vivid memories of Lingerton, old Ronnie's babbling, the ghost woman, the text, their burned-out house in Glasgow, Uncle Marty's time ghost...

The message...

The time ghost...

THE FINDING OF MAY

"Good gracious, did you get a wink of sleep?" Aunt Rosie demanded as Olly came blearily into the kitchen. "I thought the whole house was going to come down on top of us. We'll have to get Marty over. I haven't been out to see what damage there is, apart from the poor gean." She shot a glance at the window.

Olly followed her eyes and saw something very strange. Normally you looked out of the kitchen window onto the back lawn. Today all you could see was a grey tangled mass, which he stared at for a good while before he realized it was twigs. The view from the kitchen window was like looking down on the tops of trees, winter-bare trees, silver-skinned twigs, all buddy and gleaming.

"Last time we had a gale the greenhouse blew down," Aunt Rosie said, "but it was coming from the other direction that time."

A gale! A gale had blown the gean tree down so that it was lying across the lawn! It was obvious now. He was sure he had been awake all night, yet somehow he had managed to sleep through a severe gale!

Olly was never at his best in the mornings, and this morning his brain felt even more fuzzy than usual. Aunt Rosie plonked some breakfast down in front of him, then went out to inspect the damage. Olly chewed automatically, staring out of the window into what had once been the top of a tree.

The phone rang. It was Uncle Marty wondering if they were both all right. "I'll come round," he said, when Olly told him about the tree. "But I've just been on the phone to Jim Sharpe and he says his hay shed's blown down. I should go over and give them a hand, they're having a really hard time just now. You could come too, if you want. I'll be over as soon as I've managed to haul Lucy out of her pit."

"Well, there's not too much damage," Aunt Rosie announced loudly, clacking the latch on the kitchen door and slamming it shut behind her. "It's just the tree, really. Marty'll sort that."

"He phoned," Olly informed her. "He's coming over, but he wants me to go and help him up at the farm."

"What farm?"

"You know, Lower Service. The Sharpes.

Their shed's blown down."

"Oh, them," she snorted, strangely scornful. "He wastes far too much of his time on those people. You can't farm the way they do nowadays. Well, I don't know when I'm going to get my tree cleared up."

As soon as Lucy saw the tree, she announced that she would get to work on it. "I like sawing," she added, with a gleam in her eye.

They left her astride the branches, puffing away with the red bush saw, while Aunt Rosie stood nearby, watching like a cat, occasionally poking a piece of branch with her stick.

The night had been too windy for rain, but now that the gale had blown out everyone was worried that it would rain before long. There was no point in trying to repair the Sharpes' old shed, but the bales were lying exposed, scattered everywhere about the close. They had to carry them out to a clear space just outside the close and build them into piles of seventy-two bales each and then cover them with tarpaulins and tie them down with ropes and twine.

All the Sharpes joined in one by one as they came back from their various morning tasks. Olly saw Amanda working away with the others, but she never once looked in his direction. She seemed to have no trouble managing the bales by herself, but Olly found them

awkward and was glad when Ronnie appeared
and announced that he would work with him.
Everyone seemed glad about this because it
kept Ronnie out of their way. "Keep up the
good work, eh, Olly?" Jim Sharpe winked at
him as he and Ronnie passed, Ronnie blaring
away nineteen to the dozen in his ear.

They had got to the stage of covering and
tying down the last piles when Uncle Marty
sidled up behind Olly and whispered, "Make
a run for it now, kiddo – I'll keep him busy.
You know – the helmet. Try and focus in on
May: I've this hunch she's the key."

Considering what had happened the last
time he had gone up alone, Olly didn't feel too
enthusiastic about this idea, but it did seem the
perfect opportunity. No one seemed to notice
him go. Before long he was striding up past the
endless lines of rancid-smelling turnips.

He paused and looked back, a little out of
breath. Someone was standing at the bottom
of the field, watching him. Olly was pretty sure
he knew who it was – the eldest of the young
Sharpes, Adrian. He was always staring.

Olly turned and went on. He might as well.

As he came in sight of Miglo Hall he saw
there was something changed. It was the rooks
he noticed first, wheeling around in a flus-
tered, disorganized way. As he came nearer he
understood why: about half of the trees at this
end of the wood had been blown down. He

could see the grey trunks lying side by side on the ground, apart from one of them which had crashed against the building and lay propped up against the top of the wall.

There was something not right about the turret either, but he couldn't work out what until he had got almost up to it and saw its slates were gone. The roof was still there, but it was a roof of bare wooden boards, strangely pale, dry and dusty. The slates were scattered in a great swirl around the base of the wall.

Olly cracked his way over the scattered slates to the door, which was slightly open. Everything felt odd, as though something important had happened but he couldn't tell what...

He reached the top of the stair and stopped. *She* was there – the same old lady, the same pink jersey. She was standing very tall and straight, and she was talking – to old Ronnie! How was that possible? "...Must call him without delay and tell him it has been found," the stranger was saying. Her voice was incredibly posh.

Olly stared at them – and as he stared they faded. It happened just like before, except that old Ronnie faded too, and then the room faded, the window, the walls – everything faded, flickered, then seemed to return... The room was full of people – Uncle Marty, the Sharpes... The room looked different, swept and painted and clean. Again it faded. A silver mist filled everything with a faint, tangy scent which he somehow knew was the scent of bluebells in a forest on a misty forenoon in May. And then there was a voice – a woman's voice – that said, very clearly, "Are you an angel?" And a sudden shaft of light through the mist, then a whole reel of images spinning by, too jumbled to make out properly.

There was no angel. There should have been, but there wasn't. It was just a large block of pink granite with the lines of names on it, whole lines and broken lines...

How quiet Edenbridge was! Yet there were plenty of people about. And beside him was his twin, and there was May. Cautiously, he felt himself over, his hands moving down to grip the tops of his legs. He could feel that – they felt like his own legs – but they were covered with something he didn't recognize. Rough material. His legs enclosed in thick, tickly stockings. He panted slightly, softly, to stop himself gasping out loud. He was wearing a skirt, a black skirt. He felt too hot. He was itching like hell...

The War Memorial hadn't got its angel yet. It had only just been put up, and it was still a novelty that the people of Edenbridge stopped and looked at when they were passing. The pony trap was over across the road from them, Polka getting fussed by the baker's girl.

Olly blinked, and next moment the three of them were up close to the smooth pink stone, peering at the names.

"There, look," Olly's twin said suddenly. "Private Ronald Ewart, 1918."

May sniffed, but said nothing.

"It's nice, isn't it," the twin said. "It's nice they've got his name there. Look: *In memory of those who gave their lives for King and country in the Great War, 1914 to 1918. May their names never wither.*"

May glanced round, as if to check no one else was near, and then said in a low, slightly shaking voice, "It's fine and grand to be sure – and a lot of good it is to me."

The twin stared at her sharply, and Olly found he was doing the same. They were shocked, both of them, by the bitterness in May's voice. But by this time May had a handkerchief out. She gave her nose a brisk little wipe and then said, "Come away now, the pair of you, you'll be late for the school."

By the time she had finished speaking, everything had already faded again: there was mist, and sunlight and trees, and something about a campfire and caves and a holiday...

The May holiday... Here was Edenbridge again – Edenbridge crowded and jostling as even Olly had never seen it on the busiest day in modern times. That was it! It was the Whitsun market, and they had just finished their half-term holiday. He was hot and itchy because Mummy didn't believe in them changing out of their winter underclothes till the start of June, and it was still the end of May. He was wearing stockings, but a different dress this time – blue and white checks – and he was sitting in the back of the pony trap.

On holiday! They had gone away on holiday to the Wells of Dura, a tiny village where they rented a house every year with Mummy and the Pitkerro cousins – but they could look out of the bedroom window of this house across the fields and see the roofs of Lingerton, exactly a mile and a half away! *Crazy people.*

Yet the forest at Wells of Dura had been quite something: woods and waterfalls and crags and caves and acres of bluebells. You could have explored there for months and forgotten all about the world outside. It was like Disney World and the Outdoor Centre all rolled into one, except that there were just the five of them and no one told you what to do.

That was it – there was something the matter with Daddy this morning. He had been supposed to come and pick them up in the trap early, at half past seven. That was because they always went to the Whitsun market in Edenbridge before they went home after their week at Wells of Dura, and it could get quite difficult finding somewhere to leave the pony and trap. Auntie Ivy had appeared at eight o'clock and whisked the Pitkerro cousins off in their large black motor car, and then it was another hour before Daddy turned up. Mummy had told him he should be ashamed of himself, the way he looked. It seemed that that was because he had put on his second-best suit instead of his best one, and his tie was squint. The Whitsun market was one of the most important markets of the year, when they sold most of their winter-fattened beasts.

They drove slowly through Edenbridge, and Olly and his twin were all eyes. Everywhere you looked there was something going on: the streets were full of horse carts, pony traps, gigs, carriages, the odd motor car; there were crowds of people on foot, there were market stalls with red and white awnings; there were coconut-shies and sideshows; and a band in the bandstand under the trees by the river.

The master turned Polka off the road just after they had passed the new War Memorial, and they went in under an archway to a large stable yard. There was still some room there, and they left Polka and the trap with a young man who kept touching his cap and calling Daddy "Mr MacClay-sir".

Everything seemed very confused, everyone seemed very jolly, but there was definitely something wrong with Daddy. They made their way down to the cattle pens and as they wandered up and down the long lines of gates,

half deafened by the mooing and snorting of
the beasts, Olly thought he was looking more
and more ill at ease. He glanced at the other
twin and they exchanged a secretive giggle –
definitely a girls' giggle.

It was Mummy who spoke first. "And where
are the Lingerton beasts?" she demanded, in an
exceedingly suspicious voice.

"Perhaps we walked by and missed them,"
Daddy said. He was obviously trying to sound
unconcerned.

Suddenly the master of Lingerton stopped,
right in the midst of the cattle pens, slapped his
hand against his forehead and let out a roar
that, for a moment at least, made even the
cows fall silent. "May!" he exclaimed. "Oh
my goodness me!"

"May what, may I ask?" Mistress MacClay
said coldly.

He turned to her with a pleading look on his
face. "She's gone," he said in a whisper.

"Gone?"

"Last night. She went off."

"Where, in heaven's name?"

"She said she was going to France to find
her sweetheart."

"But he's dead! Ronald Ewart's dead."

"I know!" the master groaned.

"Well, she can't have got far."

"She wasn't there this morning."

"Martin MacClay," Mummy said with

terrific sternness, "what exactly has been going on?"

Olly and the other twin didn't hear what Daddy said. Mummy dragged him off a few steps out of earshot, but they could both see she was giving him a good grilling, while he stood dejectedly wringing his hands. The twins found this very funny, but they were also quaking in their black lace-up boots. Mummy was not often angry, but when she was, she was fairly terrifying.

Before they knew what was happening, she was hustling them all away from the cattle pens, away from the crowded streets and the stalls and the fun and back to the stables. There, Daddy had to practically beg the young man to let him have his pony and trap back, while the man protested, "But, Mr MacClay-sir, you're just new arrived, Mr MacClay-sir, your pony's just been given her hay, Mr Mac-Clay-sir..."

On the way home they quickly got the gist of what had happened. Daddy had been feeling so good at the end of the holiday week, because there had been no children to annoy him and no Mummy to boss him around, that he had opened a bottle of sloe wine and invited all the workers at the farm, including May, to come and try some. "It's just a country wine," they heard him say, "I had no idea it was so strong..."

Mummy snorted.

"Well, May and the girls must have put something in it to have made it so powerful," Daddy tried.

But Mummy said, "Leave *them* right out of this, if you please," in a voice that shook with menace.

Gradually Olly realized that the sloe wine was the same brew that they had picked the fruit for, back – whenever it was – the day before the day of the coffee bun. There had been no War Memorial then – it could have been years before! Did his twin look older? He wasn't sure. Possibly. Perhaps the pony trap did seem a little smaller, and that would mean they must be bigger.

It seemed that the sampling of the sloe wine hadn't stopped at one bottle. Daddy wouldn't say exactly how many had been opened, but they had a vision of the whole farm close littered with empty bottles as the men and May drank, and even danced, well into the night. The twins were delighted at this story, but they could see Mummy becoming more and more furious by the minute. The end of it all was that May had got changed into her best clothes and gone off into the night declaring she was going to fetch her true-love back. When the master had called for her the next morning, there had been no sign of her. Nor had there been any sign of the cattle, which had been in a pen in the farm close, ready to be driven to the market. It was obvious that when Daddy had woken up that morning he had been hoping that the shameful goings-on had all been a dream and that the reason there was no May, and no cows, was that they had already gone on ahead to Edenbridge.

"Stupid girl," Mummy said, several times. "Stupid girl."

They heard Daddy trying to calm her down by saying, "It's hard for her, losing her young man," but Mummy simply snapped back, "Then there was no need to make it any harder for her by forcing strong drink down her throat. And where is she now, that's what I want to know? It's not right, a young girl out wandering around the country."

Ahead they could see the trees that hid the farmhouse at Lingerton. The countryside looked very different from the way Olly knew it in modern times. Nicer – shaggier somehow, more untidy. There seemed to be more birds. Just over to the left there was a small wood, mainly of pine trees, but behind the pine trees there loomed up a large bright-leafed tree – with leaves that seemed almost to shine in the sunlight – which Olly vaguely thought he recognized.

Baldinnie ... Lingerton ... a large beech tree...

That's my mam's tree! That's where they found my mam when she went off to look for my dad. Of course!

"Stop!" he shouted suddenly. And Polka stopped, even before Daddy had reined her in. Everyone turned to look at him – at her, that was. "She's in that wood," he – she – explained.

Everyone turned and looked at the wood.

"How do you know?" Daddy enquired.

"I – I just know," Olly said.

"Can we go and fetch her?" the other twin burst out. "Please?"

They scampered down a short track into the trees and ran through the spacious shadow under the high pine branches, while Olly steered towards the bright beech tree.

"Oh," the other girl gasped as they came closer. "How did you know?"

May was there, sitting with her back to the tree, staring away over the fields. They were almost up to her before she turned and saw them.

She looked shocked, really shocked, when she did. Her hand flew up to her throat. "Oh my," she murmured. "Oh my." But at the same moment Olly was distracted by a slight movement of her other hand, as if she had swiftly pulled her hat over something lying beside her on the ground.

"May, you're not going away to leave us,

107

are you?" Olly's twin said. "You're not going away to Flanders, are you?"

May gazed at them for a while, and then suddenly large tears began to roll down her cheeks. "No," she said at length, in a tiny voice. "No, I'm not. I couldnae leave my lassies. Anyroads I cannae, for my leg's stuck doon a hole." She turned away again, looking over the fields. "I've been stuck here the hale nicht," she said. "And oh – I've seen things... But I'll never get to France, not now."

Olly felt a lump in his throat. Peeping round, he saw the other twin had tears in her eyes. Crossly, he brushed tears from his own eyes. This wasn't him crying, it was *her,* this flaming girl – whoever she was, Olive or Rosemary. Now the three of them were blubbering away, all together!

He blinked. A silence fell. His eyes were full of misty shapes again. Was that just because of the tears? There was someone in front of him ... May, standing holding her hat?

No, old Ronnie, standing holding the helmet. "Olly," Ronnie was saying, "that's my hat." He looked puzzled. They were in the turret-room again, dusty and deserted as it had been when he had found Ronnie and Mrs Hope talking together, just – when? Minutes ago? Days ago? Was he here, or was he still somewhere else? He grabbed his legs again. Did that feel like him? What did he feel like, anyway? Cautiously, he peered down at himself.

Trainers. Not lace-up boots. He was back. He turned round. There was Uncle Marty standing at the top of the stairs. No sign of Mrs Hope.

"Olly – were you in here with poor old Ronnie's helmet?" Uncle Marty demanded, pretend-angry. "I'm surprised at you! See what you've done, Ronnie, letting him have shots of it? The poor lad's hooked on it now!"

"He's not hooked, Marty," old Ronnie returned, carefully looking under the helmet and at Olly's hair.

Realizing with an effort that Uncle Marty was trying to help him, Olly grinned feebly. "I'm sorry, Ronnie," he said, "I couldn't resist."

Old Ronnie immediately grinned back at him. "It's good, Olly, isn't it? I like it too. I talk to my mam."

"There's food at the Sharpes, if you want to come down," Uncle Marty announced.

"Have you just come in just now?" Olly asked Ronnie.

Ronnie ignored him. "Dinner-time is it, Marty?" he bawled. "That's good. I wonder what we'll get? I like mince and tatties, do you, Olly?"

WHEN A BOOK ISN'T A BOOK

As Ronnie was lumbering along beside them most of the way down the track, Olly couldn't tell Uncle Marty much more than that the third experiment with the helmet had been a spectacular success. "It's getting better each time I do it," he said. "I was right *there* this time, it was really weird."

Uncle Marty said "Wow," but that was all there was time for.

Olly felt strangely confused, out of time with the real world. Mists seemed to blow through his mind now and then, as if everything was on the point of fading again, to become somewhere else, some time else. Even when there were no mists he was puzzling over what had happened, and what the link was between the Mrs Hope ghost, and Ronnie, and Lingerton. They were halfway through lunch before he realized he was sitting

110

next to Amanda Sharpe.

He immediately started feeling awkward. He could see she was doing her best to ignore him, but that might have been because she thought he had been trying to ignore her. Then, just as they were about to start eating their pudding, both of them looked up together and caught each other's eye.

It was a difficult moment. Olly somehow felt he ought to speak, and he said the first thing that came into his head. "Did you know Mrs Hope?"

"Who's that?" Amanda asked.

Olly was so surprised that he looked down and didn't say anything more. This seemed to suit Amanda too, and that was the end of their conversation, though it wasn't the end of his thinking about it – in fact, it seemed to drive all thoughts about Lingerton and ghosts out of his mind.

As they drove away from the farm, he said, "Is she stupid or what? That Amanda Sharpe. She didn't even know who Mrs Hope was."

"Ignorance isn't the same as stupidity, kiddo," Uncle Marty said gently. "I don't think she's stupid."

"But she must know who Mrs Hope is!" Olly protested. "She must know who owns the place they live in!"

"Have a think about it," Uncle Marty said. "Mrs Hope disappeared forty years ago. I don't think Amanda's quite that old yet! Didn't it occur to you she might have thought you were talking about a different Mrs Hope? Otherwise, she must have thought it was a pretty daft question, you must admit. How could she have known Mrs Hope?"

"Oh God!" Olly flushed crimson and buried his head in his hands. What was the matter with him? Every time he saw her he asked her a stupid question – and then thought she was stupid instead!

"Why were you talking about Mrs Hope with Amanda?" Uncle Marty wanted to know.

Olly gulped, and grabbed at the chance of forgetting about Amanda. "I saw her again, just before I was at – you know."

"Yeah? Where? What was she doing?"

"She was in the helmet-room place; she was talking to old Ronnie. She was telling him he had to call someone and say something had been found."

"Something? What?"

"I don't know."

This news excited Uncle Marty so much he practically drove the car into the ditch. "So old Ronnie was talking to his Auntie Betty," he murmured, after he had got the driving under control again.

"I suppose so," Olly said. It certainly all seemed to fit. "But what do you think she meant? What's been found?"

"Who knows, man? The Living Book?"

"We don't know what it is though," Olly objected.

"We could deduce," Uncle Marty said. "Start with something that has been found. OK, what's been found?"

"What, do you mean that text? That embroidery thing?"

"I hadn't thought of that," Uncle Marty admitted. "No – that's never really been lost, so you can't really say it's been found."

"What, then?" said Olly. "Oh – not that bit of paper again!"

"Well, why not? It's been lost a long time, hasn't it?"

Olly couldn't really understand why Uncle Marty kept coming back to it. "You're not saying *it's* this Living Book?" he laughed.

"Well, not the bit of paper exactly. But the way it fell, you know? OK, I know you don't like messages, it's cool. But I've been thinking, you know... You have to ask yourself what a book really is. I mean – any book: what's it for?"

Olly shrugged. "Stories. Information, like an encyclopaedia. School stuff..."

"But why write this stuff down?"

"You could put it on disk," Olly said.

"Yeah, but that's just another sort of book. Why do you need books in the first place?"

"OK," Olly said, "so you don't forget stuff."

"Right on!" Uncle Marty thumped the steering wheel enthusiastically, and the car wobbled everywhere. "It's a kind of memory. But you see, the memory that gets written in the book *isn't the same* as the thing that the memory's about – that's the real thing, the living thing, the thing you'll never find in a book."

"OK," Olly agreed.

"It's like Ma and her stories," Uncle Marty went on. "You could write her memories down and make them into a book. But you've been *living* in her memories, right? And that's different. Those are living memories. Now, if you want to get at living memories, you need a living book to do it."

"I got at them with the helmet," Olly said. "Do you mean it's the living book?"

They were nearing Rothes now, but the car was moving very slowly, as if Uncle Marty was using some of its power for thinking with.

"I don't know," he said. "I don't know if I even mean that. I mean, like, a something – a mind, out there, that *knows stuff*."

"What, this time ghost?"

This time Uncle Marty didn't tell Olly to forget about the time ghost. "Yeah," he said. "Yeah. The time ghost. Whatever it is. And, like, it's been focusing in, from way outside time – from the other side of eternity – it's been, like, trying to focus in on something, because it's trying to tell us something. OK? So let's say it's May that it's trying to focus on – May on that morning when they found her in the wood. OK, now why did she get lost in the first place?"

"Because they'd all got pissed," Olly said.

"I wouldn't put it that way if we ask Ma about it," Uncle Marty advised. "But fair enough. Now, *sloe wine* – what does that suggest to you?"

"I don't know, like what?"

"Well, think about that other time – with the coffee bun. Old Grandpa MacClay had to drive the twins into Edenbridge because May couldn't. Why? Because she was trying to get the water boiled to make the sloe wine. And she and the twins had picked the sloes on the day before."

"OK, so?"

"Well, don't you see – *that* could be the real connection. Sloes. Maybe, all the time, this thing's been trying to focus in on May, on this particular day; but, like, it's got a long way to come from – well, I don't know where the other side of eternity is, but it sounds like a long way, OK? – and it just missed, the other time. It was looking for *sloes,* and it got *picking sloes* instead of *drinking sloe wine.*"

"Like it was searching on the Internet and put in the wrong keywords!" Olly suggested.

"Well," Uncle Marty said doubtfully,

"whatever turns you on. I don't know much about the Internet."

"OK, right," said Olly. "This thing that's looking stuff up on the Internet – is that the Living Book, or the time ghost?"

"Those're just words," Uncle Marty said. "It's what it's *doing* that's important. Say it's the time ghost. Right? Say it's using living memories so that you can pick up on the thing it's trying to tell you. And, you know? Maybe that's why you never know which twin you are – because you can only live in the memories which *both twins had together*. You see? Maybe the time ghost is using the twins' memories like a bridge between out there and here – it can do that because one of the twins is already out there – Olive, she's dead, right? But one of them's still here. So it's using their memories to get this message across, into time…"

"But *what* message?" Olly almost screamed.

They had reached Burnside House. Uncle Marty parked the car and turned the engine off. "Search me," he said. The quiet *ank-ank-ank* of Lucy's saw could be heard. "What the hell." He shrugged. "Come on, Ma won't get a moment's peace till every last twig's been cleared up off her lawn."

At teatime, Uncle Marty asked Aunt Rosie if her father had ever made sloe wine. The story had never come up before, but she was off the moment he mentioned it.

"Oh yes," she chuckled, and the faraway look came into her eyes. "My father did make some sloe wine once – well, he wasn't really the one who made it, he just put the corks in the bottles. It was us who picked the berries, and May – that was the housemaid – who made the brew. They didn't drink it till years later, and it'd got very strong by then. My father got all the farm workers to try some, and May too, and oh, what a to-do! May went marching off into the night and got lost and sprained her ankle, and all the cattle went missing. My mother was terribly cross. She didn't approve of alcoholic drinks for women.

"I remember she and May quarrelled a lot around that time – just before my father died. My mother said May was dreaming instead of getting her work done. Oh dear me yes, and then she blamed it on the sloe wine and made my father throw away all that was left of it. She said it had affected May's brain and made her fanciful. Poor May. More likely what started her off was when they put up the War Memorial in Edenbridge. I think she missed her young man terribly. So many of them were killed. In the end she left Lingerton and got other work. She and my mother didn't make up again until later, after we'd moved to Rothes and May's granny had put her out. My mother was very fond of May deep down, you know, even though they quarrelled..."

Olly and Uncle Marty were set to do the dishes, and they got on very slowly because Uncle Marty wanted to continue their pondering. Olly was quite glad he didn't go back to the subject of messages but started picking carefully over all the details of Olly's experience that morning.

However, they were into the cutlery before the full force of what had really happened hit them. It had seemed so ordinary at the time that Olly had scarcely given it a second thought. It was only when you stopped to consider that it was utterly impossible.

"How did you know you would find May in that wood?" Uncle Marty asked suddenly.

"It was obvious," Olly replied promptly. "Ronnie had roared about his Mam's tree that time, remember, and – *oh my God...*"

"Exactly," Uncle Marty said. "Fine *you* knowing about that tree, but the twelve-year-old MacClay twins shouldn't have known – whichever one of them it was."

There was a long silence, before Olly breathed, "Man, that's awesome..."

"It was you, kiddo," Uncle Martin said. "*You* were there – Olly Whitman – sorting out that little problem for them seventy years before you were even born. You were born a part of history! It's a time loop, yeah? No one else knew about May's tree – they were only able to find her there because you had heard the story of how they found her there. A perfect loop – no beginning, no end..."

"I've got to get up there again!" Olly exclaimed.

"Why?"

"To try the helmet on again, of course!"

"Hey, keep your knickers on," Uncle Marty laughed. "Why are you so keen to do it?"

"I've got to find out more – I've got to find out what she put under her hat. Right? You said yourself – that's the key to all this."

"Whoa!" Uncle Marty said. "I said *May* was the key! It was probably just some old love-letter she'd been reading."

"Uncle Marty, weren't you listening to Aunt Rosie just now? Something *happened* to May that night. She found something, met someone – I don't know. And you know what? It's a bit weird about Ronnie getting born, isn't it, and May telling him that Ronald Ewart was his dad when he couldn't possibly have been. Why would she do that? Did she go a bit mad after drinking the sloe wine? Or did something else happen to her?"

"What kind of thing?" Uncle Marty looked as baffled at Olly's reasoning as Olly had felt about Uncle Marty's – yet it seemed so obvious.

"Well, like – look," Olly said. "I've been

back in time, haven't I? You said so yourself.
So if I can do it – why shouldn't she?"

"I don't know if you went back in time,"
Uncle Marty said slowly. "Something did –
but was it necessarily you?"

"Oh, come on, Uncle Marty!" Olly burst
out. "Why do you have to make everything so
complicated. It's obvious I did – and it must be
the helmet that lets you do it – and May could
have got hold of it..."

"Bit big to slip under a hat, isn't it?" Uncle
Marty objected.

"It was a big hat – a big straw thing. It might
have been covering it already, and she just
pulled it down to make sure. See, like – the
other thing is, why did old Ronnie want to go
up to live at Miglo Hall? I mean, it's a pretty
weird place to want to live."

"Maybe it was the only place he could find
where he could live in peace," Uncle Marty
said.

"Maybe he knew the helmet was there,"
Olly argued. "I mean, maybe the twins had it
after May left Lingerton, and took it up there
with them."

"No," Uncle Marty put in. "No, that can't
be right. The helmet came off an old suit of
armour that was already there at Scotservice
Tower."

"That's what Aunt Rosie says," Olly said.
"But we don't really know if she remembers

stuff right, do we? I mean, her memory's pretty gloopy, isn't it? Uncle Marty, I've got to get up there and try the helmet on again."

Uncle Marty sighed. "OK, kiddo. Maybe you're right. We'll go up first thing tomorrow. But I think you're barking up the wrong tree."

"At least what I'm saying makes sense," Olly muttered.

INTO BATTLE

"What's that racket?" Uncle Marty asked as they made their way next morning round the side of Miglo Hall, under a cohort of restless crows.

"Someone thumping and screaming, it sounds like," said Olly.

They came round the corner, and there was old Ronnie, bellowing like an enraged elephant, leaping on the scattered roof slates, flinging them wildly about.

"Stay here," Uncle Marty said to Olly. "No point in us both getting kissed by a flying slate."

As Uncle Marty went over, old Ronnie turned and seemed to take a few seconds to recognize him. Then he did, and ran to him to get a hug. It looked as though poor Uncle Marty was getting crushed to death. Olly left the shelter of the wall and went over to them.

It was a long while before Ronnie would quieten enough for them to understand him. Even after he had stopped roaring, he was so shaken by sobs and snivels that no proper words would come out. But it was not long before the awful truth was clear: his "hat" was gone. "It's stolen, Marty!" The howling broke out afresh. "Someone's come and stolen my hat!"

"Adrian Sharpe," Olly said at once. "He watched me coming up here yesterday."

"I saw Adrian today," old Ronnie sobbed. "I was having my breakfast. I saw him. He went past outside. Adrian doesn't know about my hat."

"He might have followed Olly yesterday and watched you, Ronnie," Uncle Marty said. "Adrian's always got his eyes open."

"He's always staring at you," Olly muttered. Why, why did this have to happen? He knew he ought to be sorry for Ronnie, but that wasn't the main thing to him: the main thing was that they needed the helmet. Why couldn't this have happened tomorrow? Or even in the afternoon? It wasn't fair.

"Come on, let's see Adrian Sharpe," Uncle Marty announced.

"Do you think he'd tell us?" Olly said. "Go and raid his room, more like."

"He'll tell us," Uncle Marty said firmly. "Or if he doesn't, his father will. Jim Sharpe wouldn't stand for this. Come on, Ronnie."

They found their suspect in one of the byres, pushing a barrow brimming with sloppy dung. He greeted them cheerily, which was suspicious for a start, as Adrian Sharpe was never cheery.

"Can I have a word, Adrian?" Uncle Marty said, going up to him. Olly had not noticed before how tall Adrian was. He was as tall as his father, and nearly as broad. Uncle Marty only came up to his chin.

"Ronnie has this old helmet," Uncle Marty began. "I don't know if you've ever seen him with it."

Adrian Sharpe put his head on one side and gave a puzzled frown. "What kind of a helmet's that now?" he said.

"It's like an old soldier's helmet," Uncle Marty said. "A bit of a scabby old thing."

"Oh?" Adrian Sharpe gazed away as if thinking hard. "Cannae say I've ever seen him wearing a helmet," he said at length. "Was it his dad's, or what? He's aye going on about his dad."

Just then old Ronnie butted in. "It was mine, Adrian, it wasn't my dad's. It's my hat. Give it back!"

Adrian Sharpe, still holding the barrow handles, smiled thinly and looked down at his stained overalls and the green-brown slop in the barrow in front of him. "No helmet here," he said. Then one of his arms seemed to waver slightly, and some of the dung brimmed out over one corner and went slop-plop-plop on the cobbled floor.

"Ronnie's upset, Adrian," Uncle Marty said hastily. "Never mind it. I'll ask your dad."

"Is this what you're wanting to ask me about, Marty?" a voice came, and one of the low, woodwormed doorways was filled with the tall form of Jim Sharpe, holding up Ronnie's helmet in one hand.

Olly could see Uncle Marty was taken aback. Somehow, none of them had thought that Adrian would steal the helmet and take it straight to his father. Uncle Marty did his best. "That's the one!" he exclaimed. "Where did you find it, Jim?"

"Well, I didn't exactly find it," the farmer said quietly. "Adrian here, he brought it to me. He was thinking there might be a bit of interest in it. What was it you were showing me here, Adrian?"

Adrian put his barrow down and took the helmet, turning it over carefully. "It's not First World War, that," he said softly.

"Well, that's obvious," Uncle Marty said.

"Old, is it, Marty?" Adrian Sharpe said, glancing up shrewdly.

"I don't know," Uncle Marty lied. "Could be, I suppose."

125

"Copper." Adrian Sharpe said the word slowly, heavily. "I wonder when they last wore copper helmets, now? I've been doing a bit of thinking, you see. It's not just *old*, this old helmet, is it? It's more what you would call *ancient*."

"Who knows?" Uncle Marty shrugged. "Ronnie doesn't care – he's attached to it, that's all."

"Thing is, Marty" – it was Jim Sharpe speaking now – "if Adrian here's right, then this could be worth a bit and, well, you know what our position is. The rent due and the man Savidge wandering about thinking what he'll do with the place once he's gotten rid of us. It's maybe time we had a bit of luck. What do you think it'd be worth, Marty? Hundreds? Thousands?"

"I don't know, Jim – I don't know what its value would be."

"Come on now, Marty, you're an educated man. Take a guess."

"Jim, I don't know. That's the truth. Maybe it would be valuable. But look, it's Ronnie's. He needs it, right?"

"But is it his?" Jim Sharpe persisted.

"Yes, it's mine!" Ronnie shrieked suddenly, and lunged forwards at Adrian. But Adrian sidestepped and tripped him as he was off balance, sending him sprawling onto the hard floor. Tears came welling into the old man's eyes. "It's mine," he wailed, "give it back! It makes me feel good, I can talk to my mam – give it me!"

Olly felt a surge of anger.

"What's up with everyone?" Uncle Marty muttered. "Jim, are you just going to let him trip an old man up?"

"Adrian never tripped him," Jim Sharpe growled. "The silly old bugger tripped over his own feet."

"You've always been so good to him," Uncle Marty said. "If it's his, you can't just take it away from him."

"*If* it's his, Marty, as you say," Jim Sharpe answered steadily. "But it's not. How would Ronnie come by a thing like this? Now, the Hopes of Miglo Hall, that's a different matter; they had a lot of stuff like this by all accounts. Ronnie would have found this lying about and picked it up. Oh, I'm no saying he stole it. But it belongs to the Hopes, and the Sharpes rent this land from the Hopes – so we'll just take charge of the thing."

"You can't sell it then," Uncle Marty said, "if it belongs to the Hopes."

"If old Mrs Hope was around," Jim Sharpe said, "I wouldna be getting chucked out of the farm where I was born and bred. But Mrs Hope's not around, and we're left to deal with these Crookes and Savidges that speak for her. We just have to do what we can to help ourselves. Which means you needna concern yourself about this helmet any longer – and if you dinnae like it, you can just keep off this land. I'll not deny you've always been a good friend, but I cannae abide interference."

"Jim, I'm not trying to interfere," Uncle Marty said. "I don't want you to lose your farm. But Ronnie – someone needs to stick up for him, right? You can't do this."

"All right, Marty, I'll tell you what," Jim Sharpe said suddenly, smiling a small crooked smile. "I'm a fair man. I'll fecht you for it. If you can make me sit down in that barrow, Ronnie gets his helmet. If I make you sit down in it, the Sharpes keep it."

There was a strained silence. It was a horrible situation, but Olly trusted Uncle Marty. Uncle Marty would fight and give it his best shot. Uncle Marty wasn't very big, but then right was on his side, so he had a chance. "Go on, Uncle Marty," he whispered, clenching his fists.

"No, Jim." Uncle Marty's voice cut through his thoughts. "No, we don't settle things by fighting. Look at me anyway, look at you: you think it'd be a fair fight?"

"I'll put an arm behind my back," Jim Sharpe replied promptly. "Word of honour, I'll keep it there." He began to advance towards Uncle Marty.

But Uncle Marty held his hands up. Now he

was laughing. "No, Jim," he said, "we can't settle things like this. I'm a man of peace. Call me a coward if you like, I won't fight." He was stepping backwards as Jim Sharpe came on.

"Go on, Marty, smack him," Ronnie said gleefully. He was rubbing his hands together and seemed to have forgotten all about his tears.

"Aye, I do call you a coward," Jim Sharpe said, "if you're not man enough to put your jukes up and fight for what you believe in. Come on! Hit me! Show me what you're made of!"

"Go on, Uncle Marty," Olly murmured. All Uncle Marty needed to do, he realized, was keep Jim Sharpe occupied for a few moments. Adrian's attention would be distracted and then he would be able to nip in, grab the helmet, and make off with it. He was sure he would be able to run faster up the hill than either of the Sharpes. Then, even if Ronnie didn't get it again, at least he would have a chance to put the helmet on once more!

"Stop, Jim!" Uncle Marty's voice came. He still sounded ready to laugh. "I'm not fighting – whatever you call me. Right – that's it then. We're cool. Come on, Ronnie, leave them the helmet – just leave it. Forget it."

"But Marty—" Ronnie began, his mouth dropping open.

"No," Uncle Marty stopped him. "*No way.*

129

Leave it. Come on, Olly."

Jim Sharpe had stopped advancing. Olly felt rooted to the spot. He could see old Ronnie about to obey Uncle Marty. Unbelievably, it was over. Uncle Marty turned away from Jim Sharpe, but as he did so his foot touched the slop which had spilled out of the barrow. It seemed to happen in slow motion, Uncle Marty's foot slipping out from under him, how he put his hands out to break his fall, at the same time twisting and finishing up on his knees, but up to his armpits in the brown-green ooze in the barrow.

"Ah well, there's justice somewhere," Jim Sharpe said, turning back to the doorway he had come out of.

When Olly next looked, Adrian and the helmet had gone too.

Uncle Marty hoisted himself upright, holding his dripping arms out. "I'll drive you home if you like, Olly," he grinned. "If you can stand the smell."

Something inside Olly snapped. It was the grin that did it. "Do you mean that's it?" he said.

"Looks like it, kiddo," Uncle Marty responded.

"God," Olly said. He was nearly speechless, beside himself with anger. "God... No wonder my mum..." He gulped. Tears of rage and disappointment were filling his eyes. Everything his parents had said about Uncle Marty was true. "You know, you're a real wimp – you're such a total loser," he said, blurting the words out through his tears. "Well, you can piss off, OK? I wouldn't go in the car with you anyway. I'm finished with you." And he set off at a run, out of the close and down the hill.

Uncle Marty called after him a couple of times but he ignored it. He meant what he had said.

MAUDIE
TAKES CONTROL

Five months passed, and Olly had no more contact with Uncle Marty. He didn't change his mind about what he had said; he didn't relent. Whenever he thought about him he felt furious. *Time ghost! Living Book!* Uncle Marty hanging off the edge of the planet, more likely! The man really was a waste of space.

Christmas was the most miserable Olly could remember. They had moved into a rented house that none of them really liked. "It stinks of baby puke," Maudie muttered. It was also damp, with mould growing on one of the bathroom walls, and it was even smaller than their old house.

But it was the smallness of the new house that caused things to change again. There were only two bedrooms, and that meant Olly and Maudie had to share. Maudie did her best to pretend Olly didn't exist, and one of the first things she did was to string up an old sheet down the middle of the room to divide it. Olly's side was furthest from the window.

One night he woke up suddenly and saw the sheet twitching, then the bottom of it was lifted and Maudie's head appeared under it. "Why did you never tell me?" she said.

"Tell you what?" Olly asked.

"About going up to that old house and meeting that old guy."

Olly thought. "Uncle Marty asked me to go – to begin with," he said.

"And I got left with juicy Lucy with the sparkling smile," Maudie said.

"Lucy's all right."

"So's cake icing," Maudie answered. "But it doesn't mean you want it all the time."

"I'm sorry," Olly said. "I didn't mean to leave you out."

"I wouldn't have set the house on fire if you hadn't," Maudie said.

"What!" Olly exploded.

"Think about it," Maudie said. Then her head was withdrawn.

"I already have," Olly called through the sheet. "Haven't had a chance to think about much else, in case you hadn't noticed."

"Then think harder," Maudie's voice came, muffled.

What did she mean? Olly *had* thought, and the only kind of explanation he had come up with was that Maudie was mad. It wasn't much of an explanation, but it was better than nothing.

But whatever she had meant when she told him to think harder, from that night Maudie seemed more ready to talk to Olly. He, in turn, began to tell her about the things he most needed to speak about – Uncle Marty and the helmet and old Ronnie and Lingerton and the ghost of Mrs Hope. And Maudie listened with growing interest.

She got very agitated when he told her about the helmet. She said Uncle Marty was a total jerk, and wanted to march straight off to Fife and set fire to the Sharpes' barns. Olly reminded her she'd already caused enough trouble with fires, which made her flap her arms about with irritation so that the dividing sheet came down on top of her. She struggled free. "I can't do anything to put it right," she said, "so I might as well have the fun of starting another fire."

"Do you think it was fun?" Olly asked, shocked.

"Sure it was," she said. "I think fires are really cool."

Maudie didn't put the sheet up again, which certainly made life pleasanter in their bedroom, though she did take to getting dressed and undressed in the bathroom, which annoyed all the rest of the family.

Gradually Olly told her about all his strange experiences. Maudie was fascinated. She asked question after question, going back over details again and again. Even the things Olly didn't much want to remember were wormed out of him – like the weird woollen underwear, and if it felt any different being a girl, and what it was like going for a pee.

For weeks Maudie simply listened, without making any suggestions. But one afternoon just after Easter, when they had come home from school together, she picked up on something which Olly had forgotten about.

"The third time you went to put the helmet on," she said, "you didn't, did you?"

"I don't remember putting it on," Olly said. "But it really messes with your head, so that doesn't mean anything. When I came back from … wherever, Ronnie was standing in front of me and he looked like he'd just taken it off me – so I must have put it on."

"How do you know he wasn't just holding it?" Maudie persisted.

"I saw him there when I first went in," Olly objected.

"But it couldn't have been him really, could it? Because you'd left him down with Uncle Marty and the Sharpes."

"I don't know," Olly said. "What does it matter anyway? It's gone."

"I'll tell you what it matters," Maudie said.

135

"It matters because you've been sitting here sulking for the last six months, when you could have just gone over to Fife again and tried to get one of your visions *without* the stupid helmet! I mean, for God's sake, you managed to see that old woman without it."

"She was different—"

"Crap! You're just a wally. Listen, suppose Uncle Marty is right about you getting a message? Well, a message has got to come from someone, or something, hasn't it?"

"I suppose so."

"So, the something that's sending the message is this time ghost, right?"

"Yes, but I don't know what that is. Uncle Marty doesn't either. He said it wasn't anything. It was just a word he made up."

"Exactly," Maudie said. "But it was a word he made up to describe something. The time ghost doesn't mean a real ghost or anything – it just means the way everything's connected." Maudie, who was sitting cross-legged on her bed, raised one hand in a V-sign and put on a stupid grin. "*Hey, love and peace – like, everything's connected, right?*" she crooned, rolling her eyes.

Olly giggled. She had got Uncle Marty just right. But now Maudie's smile faded and she told him sternly, "It's nothing to do with the helmet. There's a message, but you're not getting it because you're missing the connections."

"But what connections?"

"OK, try this," she said. "Remember, that time after the fire, you went with Mum to Number 29 to pick up your stuff?"

"I wanted to get that book of Dad's before he found it was missing," Olly replied.

"Exactly," Maudie said. "And you saw those things – the plaster coming off the wall and the pattern the smoke had made, like branches?"

"OK."

"Right, that plaster coming off the wall – doesn't it make you think of anything?"

"No."

"It's just as well I've been listening to you," Maudie said. "Listen to me, numbat. When you told me about how you came up to Miglo Hall that day after the gale, you said that what you noticed was the queer way the wood looked where the slates had come off the roof – 'all pale and dry', that's what you said."

"Right…"

Maudie went on. "Think. Miglo Hall: trees down, pale and dry wood – underneath-wood."

"OK."

"Now, think. Number 29: tree pattern; underneath-wood – where the plaster had come off. Extra ingredient: Dad's book."

"You just keep talking, Maudie," Olly grinned. "But don't forget you're supposed to be starting the tea."

"You just keep listening," Maudie snarled, "and thank your stars you've got a sister like me – so patient and kind. Remember when Aunt Rosie got you to hack down that bush in front of the garage window?"

"Right," said Olly.

"Don't you get it? More branches. And what did you do that same afternoon, up in the loft?"

"Sorted books," Olly said, "but—"

"Right, old books again. Get it yet? Number 29: one, tree pattern; two, plaster off and underneath-wood; three, old book. Burnside House: one, tree branches; two, old books; three, well, the loft's falling to bits, so there must have been lots of plaster off and under-neath-wood there. Then, Miglo Hall: one, trees down; two, slates off and underneath-wood; three, sure, you didn't see an old book, but you saw the ghost in the library that time, so that's almost the same thing. You see? It's the same pattern: there's a message in these events!"

Why did everyone talk about messages? Olly could see some dim sense in what Maudie was saying – but too dim... He gazed at her. No, Maudie had definitely flipped. He was sharing a room with a lunatic.

"So?" she demanded. "Did you see plaster coming off a wall in the loft or not?"

"In the loft? I don't know! I wasn't looking." Olly was as confused as ever, but there was a faint glimmer of light in Maudie's ranting. Perhaps she hadn't flipped. Something about things belonging together – *everything's connected* – tree-branches and underneath-wood and books... There was a sort of pattern... *"That's the place where books kept falling through and disappearing,"* he murmured.

"What?" Maudie snapped.

"It's what Aunt Rosie said!" Suddenly he leaped off his bed, slapped his hand across his head, spun round and grabbed Maudie by the shoulders. "Yes!" he yelled.

"Get off." Maudie shook him loose. "Yes what?"

"Plaster!" he beamed at her. "Not in the loft – in the garage! When I got the bike out, I hit my head, so I punched it and the plaster fell off – there were wood bits under the plaster! I looked up into that bit between the walls, right? The bit where books fell through and got lost; I saw a book, that's what it was! It was stuck in the wall! I saw it, Maudie – it was there all the time! You're a genius, Maudie!"

"OK," said Maudie calmly, "and it was staring you in the face, so you're an idiot. There's just one small problem. We're sitting here in the middle of Glasgow; and that book – which the poor old time ghost has been trying like crazy to tell you about – is stuck inside a wall over in Fife."

"What'll we do?" said Olly.

Maudie considered. "We're going to go over," she said.

"When?"

"Now."

"But—"

"Come on," she said, "Mum'll be home any minute. I don't have any cash though, you'll have to pay for us both on the bus."

"Maudie!"

"I can't help it. They won't give me pocket money any more, remember? We've got to get over and see this thing, haven't we? So, get your piggy-bank open, let's get moving."

Three hours later, they were stepping off the bus at Kinross. Dusk had fallen. Kinross was quiet and empty and foreign-seeming. The orange street lights glowed strangely.

"Right, now you phone Uncle Marty," Maudie said.

"Maudie!"

"What?"

"Last time I spoke to him I called him a loser!"

"So? It's time you said sorry, isn't it?" She grabbed Olly by the shoulders and propelled him across the road into a phone box.

It didn't take Olly long to realize Maudie

was more determined than he was. He sighed, and fished out the rest of his money – a couple of ten pence pieces. It was odd how he could remember Uncle Marty's number so easily.

"Hey, it's been such a long time!" Uncle Marty greeted him. He sounded as friendly as ever.

Olly mumbled something in reply.

"So, what are you doing with yourself?" Uncle Marty wanted to know.

"Well," Olly said, "we're at Kinross. Me and Maudie."

"Tell him about the book!" Maudie whispered fiercely.

"What are you doing in Kinross?"

"I – we – thought – could you pick us up, please?"

"Is Ma expecting you?"

"No, it's just, I mean, Maudie thought—"

"Your mum and dad don't know you've come either?" Uncle Marty was sounding a little more serious now.

"Not really, no – we should have left a note, shouldn't we?" Olly said.

"Maybe something would have been handy, you know?" Uncle Marty said. "You've no phone at your new pad, have you? How can I get in touch with them?"

"You could ring our neighbour," Olly suggested. Maudie shook her head ferociously.

"Right, I'll do that." Olly gave him the

number as Maudie kicked him on the shins, once for each digit. "Give me half an hour," Uncle Marty said and rang off.

They were both starving by this time, but didn't have enough money left to buy anything to eat. They sat on a bench for the next forty minutes, sulking and trying to ignore the smells from the little fish and chip shop across the road.

When Uncle Marty arrived, they learned that their parents had been going to come over and collect them, but he had managed to persuade them to let Olly and Maudie stay overnight at Aunt Rosie's. Aunt Rosie had agreed to this too. "But I warn you," he added, "Ma's not doing it out of the goodness of her heart. It's just that she hasn't seen Maudie since her little escapade – and she wants to inspect her and see if she's started sprouting horns and a forked tail. And you've got to go back first thing tomorrow morning. Now, what's this about a book?"

Uncle Marty got them a haggis supper each, and as they gratefully waded into it Maudie tried to explain about the conversation which had ended in their scurrying out of the house and off to the bus station. Olly didn't say much. He felt very uncomfortable with Uncle Marty – and Uncle Marty being so nice to him just made everything worse.

After Uncle Marty had got it all straightened

out, he said Aunt Rosie might even be interested. "So maybe she won't eat you for supper," he added.

Over the last part of the journey he brought them up to date with what had been going on around Rothes. "Poor old Ronnie isn't too great," he said. "He got really depressed after his helmet got stolen, so in the end I took him to the doctor, and the doctor gave him some pills. But these pills made him start to have bad fits again, so he had to double the pills he took for his fits – and that made him more depressed again. He hardly talks now – and he certainly doesn't see angels any more!"

"Did the Sharpes sell the helmet?" Maudie asked.

"Jim took it to some junk-shop in Edinburgh – you know, because it was stolen. He couldn't take it to a proper museum or anything. He got two thousand quid."

"Wow," Olly said, despite himself.

"You can be sure it was worth at least five times that," Uncle Marty said. "It hasn't got him out of debt, but I suppose it'll keep Crooke, Barbour and Savidge off his back for a bit. He won't be any better off in the long run. The problems'll just come back, you know?"

Aunt Rosie didn't look pleased to see them. "I don't have any food in the house," was the first thing she said when they appeared at the door. However, she couldn't resist offering them some of the Belgian biscuits she had been making, and as they ate Uncle Marty tried to explain to her that they had suddenly realized something very important and couldn't wait to come over and investigate.

Aunt Rosie looked bewildered. "A book? What sort of book? I don't know about any book."

"I think it slipped through the wall and fell down, long ago," Olly explained. He thought that was bound to ring a bell with Aunt Rosie after what she had told him.

Aunt Rosie was unmoved. "Why should it do that?" she demanded.

"Just let them go and look, Ma," Uncle Marty said. "It could be something you've forgotten about."

"I can't think what I could have forgotten about," Aunt Rosie said. "We never lost any books. Well, there's a torch over there, you'd better take that – and the garage key's in the basket on the dresser."

After that she pretended to be more interested in clearing up the table and washing the cups and plates, but as they started off towards the garage they realized from the sound of grumbling behind them that Aunt Rosie was following.

They would have got on quicker without

her, but they felt better now they had got her interest, so they patiently put up with her shining the torch in all the wrong places, and poking off round the garage muttering about all the things that needed tidying up. In the end she let Olly take the torch and shine it up into the space between the walls.

Olly shone and squinted for several minutes. "There's a book – it's wedged," he breathed eventually.

"Here's the bike pump," Maudie said.

The pump would barely fit into the gap, but there was just enough room for him to move it forwards and back. It came in contact with something, but he had to keep taking it out to peer in and see if he was getting anywhere.

Then suddenly, with a sound no louder than a scuttling mouse, and a small shower of plaster, it moved, shifted, slipped – and he had it.

It was a very small book, but quite thick for the size of it.

"The battery's down," Olly announced as they peered at the strange, thick pages without being able to make anything out. "We'll have to look at it inside."

Back in the kitchen, Aunt Rosie looked at the book blankly. "Never seen it in my life before," she muttered. "I can't make this out at all. What is it?"

They crowded round her, and saw what she meant. The pages, which were thick and greeny-grey, seemed to be blank – blank and engrained with dirt. There were some marks which might have been faint writing, but they might just as well have been grubby smudges.

Uncle Marty said, "It didn't belong to May Forester, did it?"

And suddenly Aunt Rosie said "Oh" in a way that meant she'd remembered something. "I think I know about this," she said. "Just after we came here... May asked us to bring her a book up from the loft. We went off to get it, but on the way down past the house my mother called me in for something, so Olive went to find it. But it slipped down behind the shelf and into a crack in the wall. By the time I'd got to the loft it was gone. I remember we tried to reach in but the gap was too narrow. We had to go and tell May it was gone."

"Did you not think to go and break into the wall from down below – from the garage?" Olly asked her.

"No," she laughed, "We wouldn't have thought of a thing like that. May didn't seem to mind that much, so we never really gave it another thought. She had her baby by that time, and little Ronnie was all she was interested in. She was so devoted to him; it's a shame he turned out the way he is. Fancy you finding the book again! I can't think why she should have wanted it."

A GLIMPSE FORWARDS

Uncle Marty could scarcely contain his glee. When he came back over next morning, he was practically punching the air in triumph. "This is it!" he kept saying, dancing about. "This is most definitely it. This is what the message was about!"

"It feels like soft plastic," Maudie said. "Sort of cool and... It's nice."

"It can't be plastic, though," Uncle Marty said. "Because they didn't have plastic in those days. What's it like? Skin? Frog-skin, yeah, living frog-skin."

"Yeugh! It's not!" Maudie didn't like frogs.

Uncle Marty had promised to put them on the first available bus to Glasgow, but as soon as they had pulled away from the gate of Burnside House he asked, "Anyone game for a quick visit to old Ronnie? It's just possible he might know something about this."

If they had stopped to think about it, they would have realized that Ronnie had still been a baby when the book got lost so he couldn't possibly have seen it – but they were too excited to think about such details.

They drove to Scotservice Tower and walked to Miglo Hall through the wood. Uncle Marty was carrying the book, and he and Maudie strode ahead while Olly lagged. He was feeling a bit put out that Maudie and Uncle Marty were getting on so famously.

He looked about him. It was the first time he had been at Miglo Hall for five months, and he had a strange feeling that an old part of him had been left behind here. He stopped and looked up at the slateless roof. The bared roofboards were no longer pale: already the rain and snow of the winter had soaked them to a dull brown. Probably the wet had got inside too – but that didn't matter, because old Ronnie wouldn't come here any more to talk to his mam and his Auntie Betty.

He went on to the front door. The first nettle tips were just coming up through the black soil on the floor, delicate, red-tinged. He paused again, looking over to the doorway leading off the main hall.

There was no "ghost" this time, but he stopped and stared all the same. Was that a light on? It was a sunny day, but it seemed darker in there than it should have been.

Forgetting about the others, Olly went hesitantly towards the open doorway and peered in...

Uncle Marty was there. He was sitting at a table with a reading-lamp on it. And the strangest thing was that Olly had been expecting to see him there – Olly, but not Olly. It was like that morning at Baldinnie when he had recognized May's tree, when he had been one of the twins but at the same time still himself. He was two people, only this time he was himself and another Olly.

Uncle Marty was in the *library*. He looked up when Olly came in. There was something different about him. He was still Uncle Marty, friendly and good-natured, but also – what? Not so daft, maybe. There seemed to be a lot of grey in his hair.

Uncle Marty looked up – as though he had been expecting Olly – and said, "It's amazing, you know? Forwards, backwards – from the middle outwards – you can't *see* any pattern to it, but you know there *is* a pattern. You have to get inside the pattern... You start to change..."

Olly's mouth opened, and he spoke without even meaning to. "So have you decided what it is, Marty?" *Marty*, not *Uncle Marty*.

"Olly," Uncle Marty replied, "this Book – can do anything. It could take you anywhere. *Anywhere.* Do you understand? Of course –

how do you think all this was possible?" Uncle Marty gestured around him. Half reluctantly, Olly's glance took in the bookshelves, the polished wooden floor, painted ceiling, the glass in the window... As he looked outside, the other Olly already knew what he would see...

Everything was changed. The nettles were gone, the fallen trees, the scattered slates. Where the great space of nettles had been there was a kind of courtyard with arched entrances down one side of it, cobbled paths, a lawn and flower-beds, a well in the very centre. There seemed to be a lot going on, people all over the place – a lot of young people – all busy with various things. Logs were being unloaded from a cart in front of which stood an extremely large brown horse. Was this some other vision of the past? But a young man stood beside the horse, who Olly at first thought was Adrian Sharpe. Yet it wasn't: it looked more like Robert. And the other Olly knew it *was* Robert, who was here as usual for the summer holidays although he was actually studying physics at university. This Olly also knew that the logs had been brought over from the forest on the far side of Hill of Service to be seasoned in the drying-shed. He knew that over three hundred people were living and working on the Hill of Service Estate – that was what it was called now – and that the three Estate farms – the Sharpes', and Craigenputtock and Eastridge – grew all the food for them, that Uncle Marty was in charge of everything but that Maudie did most of the organizing... He turned back to Uncle Marty.

Uncle Marty was looking thoughtful, and he patted the desk in front of him. "It's only just beginning, you know," he said. "It'll take us the rest of our lives sorting this thing out."

Olly noticed then that it wasn't the Book on the desk but just a small notepad and various odd pieces of paper scattered untidily about. Slowly, a strange new feeling – like a sudden surge of hope, of excitement – came across him. *Something* was happening, here at Miglo Hall, something that not many people knew about yet, that was waiting for its day to come when it would start changing things in a big way – for the better.

The moment passed as quickly as it had come, and he saw Uncle Marty glance up again, with a different expression on his face – like a sly grin, almost with a wink. "Of course," he said, "you realize we're not quite there yet, don't you?"

And Olly winked too and nodded. "I'll see you then," he said, turning away.

The next thing he knew, he was looking up at Maudie and Uncle Marty, who were standing over him where he was sitting on the damp ground fiddling with a piece of broken glass in the soft black earth.

"Why didn't you come in?" Uncle Marty asked. "That was really interesting."

Olly felt very confused. He shrugged and said nothing.

Uncle Marty stared at him expectantly for a moment, then he went on. "Hey – old Ronnie had one of his famous moments. In fact, I've an idea our Book brought him right back to his old self."

"What famous moments?" Olly asked vaguely.

"You know!" Uncle Marty laughed. "Like at Baldinnie – when he first saw you?"

"Yeah," Maudie put in, "he just took the Book and, like, stared at it for about five minutes, then handed it back and said, *'The angel gave this to my mam.'*"

As they drove off again Uncle Marty said, "You know what? I reckon May described this Book to Ronnie. He can't actually have seen it before. But you couldn't really mistake it, could you? She must have talked to him about it. What if..." He paused. "Like – it must have been really important to her, you know?" he went on. "I mean, by the time she started telling him bedtime stories and stuff, that must have been three or four years after the Book had got lost. But she was still thinking about it. Why?"

"A present from her boyfriend?" Maudie suggested.

"I think you're on the right track, kiddo," he said. "But what if... No."

"What?" Maudie smiled

"Well," Uncle Marty said, "you know this weird thing about how Ronald Ewart was killed six years before Ronnie was born, but Ronnie still insists he was his dad."

"Right," said Maudie.

"Put yourself in her position," Uncle Marty said. "Right – you've lost your true-love, he's been killed in the war. What would be the one thing you would wish for, if wishes came true?"

"To have him back," Maudie answered.

"Right," Uncle Marty said. "And then, suppose she got that wish – but she couldn't really, like, get it completely, because people aren't really allowed to come back from the dead, but he was, like, allowed to come back just once, or—"

"Like in *Truly, Madly, Deeply*," Maudie put in. "When he comes back, but it's only for a little while, and he's always cold and he really wants to go again..."

"Yeah," Uncle Marty said. "Yeah, something like that. And so suppose she couldn't get that one wish that she really wanted – what would be the next best thing?"

"To have a part of him," Maudie said, with relish. "To have his baby."

"Right on," Uncle Marty said.

153

"I hope you're not suggesting this is a book that makes wishes come true," Maudie grinned.

"Well..." Uncle Marty said doubtfully. "What do you think, Olly?"

Olly, in the back seat, pretended he couldn't hear. He felt more uncomfortable than ever. He knew he should tell them about the vision he had just had. That wonderful feeling of purpose, of wishes come true – everyone working together for something – and all made possible because of the Book. *This Book can do anything.* Why couldn't he just tell them?

"He thinks we're in for hell on toast when we get home." Maudie giggled. "He's too worried even to speak!"

They got to Kinross with about four minutes to spare before the bus arrived. Uncle Marty stood at the bus stop holding the Book up in front of him as if he thought the sunlight could shine through it and make everything clear. He started murmuring:

You come, imperfectly,
You are half-seen,
You are in confusion.
Your day comes; your page can be read...

"Remember that, Olly?" he asked. "It makes you wonder, doesn't it?"

Olly grunted. Of course he remembered it,

it was that text they had found in Aunt Rosie's hallstand. It was just – he couldn't talk. His mouth felt clipped shut. What was the point, anyway? Uncle Marty could work everything out with Maudie. Olly just felt stupid.

Suddenly Uncle Marty said, "Hey – here's a test. Mr Book, please let us win the lottery!" He laughed. "Take it," he said, handing it to Olly. "A magic book's going to be what you need when you get home. Show it to your dad. Let it be your talisman. I'll see it again next time. Seriously though, I hope Maudie doesn't get too much grief from your little adventure."

"I don't care," Maudie muttered.

"Hey," Uncle Marty said, giving her shoulder a gentle shake, "I know it's hard when you're being punished and you don't know when the punishment's going to stop. Try and stay cool though; they'll come round in the end. The cooler you stay, the quicker they'll come round."

SMALL POSSESSION

On a Saturday morning some time later a letter arrived, addressed to their mother. She opened it, frowning in a puzzled way. She said, "It's from Marty – peculiar…"

"What does he say?" Olly's dad asked, from behind the sports page.

"It's a cheque," she said blankly. "For fifty thousand pounds."

"What?!" Mr Whitman leaped to his feet and his newspaper scattered around like over-sized snowflakes.

"He says he's had some luck on the lottery," Olly's mother said. "He says he wants us to have this because we had such bad luck with our house."

Together, they turned to Olly.

"I don't know anything about it!" he exclaimed.

"He must have had a huge win," his dad

said. "He wouldn't be throwing fifty grand around unless he'd had one of the really big wins. I mean – millions."

Olly made a bolt for the bedroom. He shook Maudie, who was still asleep, and for once didn't get a punch in the eye for it – though how she worked out what he was trying to say was a mystery, because he was gabbling like a madman.

This time, Olly persuaded Maudie to phone Uncle Marty. "He likes you better than me now anyway," he said.

Maudie went along to the phone box at the end of the road. She wouldn't let Olly come with her, so he sat waiting feverishly on his bed, turning the Book over and over in his hands. It felt so strange: cool, without being cold, and heavy, heavier than it should have been for its size. What did it remind him of? An egg which he had found among the hay at the Sharpes' farm... The egg had had the same heavy coolness – not cold, like an egg from the fridge. What was it? The feeling that there was something inside it? Something that might hatch?

Slowly he got up, and slipped the Book into his back pocket. He decided he wasn't going to let it out of his sight again. Or was that the reason? Perhaps he did it because he thought the Book had been too cold, lying on his bedside table, and it needed to be kept warmer...

Maudie returned. Uncle Marty's phone seemed to have been cut off. She had tried phoning Aunt Rosie instead, but Aunt Rosie was still cross with her and told her she ought to wait until Uncle Marty could tell her himself. "Then she just wanted to talk about my boring exams," she complained.

"We'll have to go over there," Olly said.

"You'll stay right here," his mother replied. "I'm not having any more wild goose chases to Fife! And Maudie's got her exams to study for."

"She won't do any studying!" Olly scoffed.

"She will if she ever wants to go to Fife again," his father warned.

"Anyway, it's nothing to do with you," Mum said. "He sent the cheque to me." Shortly after that she shut herself into the living-room and got down to writing Uncle Marty a very nice letter – which must have been difficult, considering the usual way she spoke about him.

Olly thought it was high time they tried to get some use out of the Book for themselves. He persuaded Maudie to get herself done up with make-up and her leather skirt so that she looked eighteen and go and buy a lottery ticket. He gave her his last pound for this. They waited on tenterhooks till lottery night – but they were disappointed. Not even one number was right.

"It was just a coincidence," Maudie declared.

"Just pure luck."

"Why doesn't Uncle Marty's phone work?"
Olly demanded, for the hundredth time.

In no time, their parents found the posh new
house which they wanted to buy with Uncle
Marty's money. Olly didn't like it much. He
kept thinking of Miglo Hall, restored and full
of people. No excitement measured up to the
feeling he got when he thought of that. But
Mum and Dad were wandering about in a
happy dream.

Maudie's exams came closer, and when her
study leave started she suddenly declared, "I'll
only work for my exams if we can go over to
Rothes."

Their parents argued and threatened, cajoled
and promised, but they didn't have the heart
for a real fight. Maudie said she didn't care if
she didn't pass any exams. In the end they
agreed to let her and Olly go to Fife for the
long weekend. After all, they were still curious
to find out more about what had happened.

The countryside was very green and bright as
they travelled through – trees in leaf, flowers
everywhere, and a feeling of excitement in the
air, even inside the stuffy bus.

But Uncle Marty looked unchanged, as
tattered and holey as ever. He still had the
same old car. "I thought you'd have a new Merc
by now," Maudie said.

"What's that?" Uncle Marty asked.

"It's a car!"

Uncle Marty laughed and shook his head. There was something strange and secretive about him. To begin with, he wouldn't say how big his win was. In the end they got out of him that he was not a millionaire – "just a quarter of one."

"Two hundred and fifty thousand pounds – wow, cool!" Olly exclaimed, when he had worked it out. A quarter of a million didn't sound like much; two hundred and fifty thousand sounded like a fortune.

"I have to see Jim Sharpe," Uncle Marty said as they came to the Lower Service farm road. "Do you mind?"

"Are you talking to him again?" Olly exclaimed.

"Why not?" Uncle Marty laughed. "Life's too short to keep up a quarrel."

Olly wondered if he was thinking of him when he said this. Uncle Marty behaved perfectly normally towards him, but Olly had a growing feeling, which he didn't at all like, that he would never be able to speak properly to Uncle Marty again until he had apologized for the things he had said to him.

It was not until they had come up to the farm close and saw the bulldozers working where the old hay shed had blown down that the truth about Uncle Marty's money began to dawn. "What's going on here?" Maudie demanded.

"Foundations for some new farm buildings," Uncle Marty said.

"But where did they get the money from?"

"Heaven." Uncle Marty smiled.

"You didn't!" Maudie said, unbelieving. "You didn't give them money. No – you did! Are you crazy? After what they did! How much?"

"Enough," Uncle Marty said.

"Enough for what?"

"For what they need," Uncle Marty replied. "And then there were the Clydesdales. I couldn't resist the Clydesdales. Just think of it. They're really beautiful beasts, you know? It was just too far out – I had to see that happen. Horses pulling ploughs, wow, I mean..."

"How much – but – haven't you kept something for yourself? What – what..." Maudie stammered.

"Hey, I'm fine," Uncle Marty laughed. "Remember I could never make toast? I can now. I've got this really expensive toaster! I still feel a bit guilty about it, but hey, we only live once!"

Olly couldn't believe his ears. Mum and Dad had been right – Uncle Marty simply wasn't on this planet. He had won two hundred and fifty thousand pounds and he had got himself an electric toaster!

They got out of the car. Uncle Marty must have noticed they were looking shocked. "Hey," he said, "perhaps it was luck, or perhaps it really was the Book. Right now, I think it was. That's cool. Maybe we can do good things with it. But money, right – you've got to let it go. If you try to keep hold of money, you know, it just twists you up inside."

"What an idiot," Maudie muttered as they watched him walking off towards the big yellow bulldozer. "What a complete jerk."

"Come on," Olly said, "let's go on up the hill."

They left the close and the racket of the bulldozer, and started up the track that led towards Miglo Hall.

"Why didn't it work for us?" Olly wanted to know.

"Because things don't work for us," Maudie snarled. "It's just idiots like Uncle Marty they work for, and he doesn't even appreciate it. I'm fed up. I want to set fire to something."

Suddenly Olly said, *"It can't be used for evil purposes, because evil people are always liars."* The words popped out, seemingly out of nowhere.

Maudie jumped, and glanced at him, almost scared. "Don't say things like that," she said. "Why did you say that?"

"I don't know," Olly said. He felt as startled

as she was. "I don't know. I heard it somewhere..."

"I lied about my age, didn't I?" she said. "I
pretended to be over eighteen."

They walked on in silence.

"Yeah," Maudie said suddenly, "It was on
that bit of paper – the one that fell from the
sky. It must have been something about the
Book."

"Yeah," Olly agreed. "In other words, there
must have been someone at Miglo Hall who
knew about the Book."

They went on in silence.

They were almost in sight of Miglo Hall when
they heard the bang, and the second they heard
it they were running – running like hares –
towards the sound.

They rounded the corner just in time to see the
tree that the gale had left propped against the
wall flopping to the ground. They even heard
the crack of its branches. The second thing
they noticed was the clouds of black smoke.

MAY'S COTTAGE

Olly and Maudie hurtled towards the ruined house and the spire of smoke that towered above it. They had no thoughts of being heroes, or of rescuing anyone. They simply had to run. If they had been facing in the opposite direction they would probably have run back down to the farm. But they were facing Miglo Hall.

They reached the great pillared porch and stopped, peering in. Everything looked almost normal, except that the light was strange: an odd kind of twilight, moving with dappled black shadows. They went in through the doorway, and what they saw was anything but normal.

They took in every detail in a second – the red fire and black smoke pouring upwards, how the caravan's windows seemed to have disappeared, until they realized they were

164

looking at its roof because it was lying on its side. They could see the leafy branches of trees through the collapsed wall beyond it.

"Old Ronnie must be in there!" Olly screamed.

"I know!" Maudie yelled back. Tears were pouring down her face.

"I'll have to see if I can get him!" Olly yelled.

"No, you can't!" Maudie screamed back.

"You run back and get help!" Olly ordered. "Go on, go!" And he plunged forwards towards the caravan.

But before he was anywhere near it, he stopped, beaten back by the heat. He turned away, shielding his head with his arm, trying to peer back at the fearsome glow without burning his eyes. Was that a window smashed open at the end of the caravan? And was that a head just inside it? Perhaps it would be possible to reach through and grab Ronnie and drag him out...

He dropped to the ground to try and see more clearly and, as soon as he was down, the heat felt less intense. That was good! He could get closer now. He crawled forwards. He felt nettle stings and broken glass pressing against his hands, but he felt glad of the coolness of the ground. Cool ground, cool earth...

But now fire was shooting over him, zipping over him in great howling arcs. And then there was *boom – boom – boom*, like late echoes of the explosion ringing round his head, only they were getting louder, not fainter. And *zip – zip*, then *boom – boom – boom* again, nearly deafening, shaking the ground. The ground seemed to be wetter here, wonderfully cool, but mud, splodgy mud – Ronnie's water tank must have tipped over – and at each *boom* the mud seemed to ripple and gasp, as though the earth was trying to breathe. Why did the explosion keep booming? He looked up, but it was too dark to see anything. The smoke must have become too thick.

But just as he was thinking that the darkness above him was not like the darkness of smoke – *zip-boom, zip-boom* – streaks of light went tearing through it, and flashes and echoes prickled the darkness far out to either side of him. There was something wrong. The smoke, yes – the smoke was poisonous and he was hallucinating…

"Take my hand. Get up. Don't be frightened." The voice came from just behind him. A cool, brave voice…

"Maudie? Maudie, is that you? Something's happened to me, I'm—"

"Come, get up out of the mud, you can't stay there." A girl's voice, yes – but perhaps not Maudie's. And then two legs appeared just in front of his eyes. Not girl's legs though: horse's legs. *Oh God*. He hid his eyes in his muddy hands.

166

There was a soft exclamation, then a soft splodging. A moment later he was taken by the shoulder and shaken. "Come on, get up." There was impatience in the voice now. "We have work to do."

Olly uncovered his eyes. There was a pair of human legs now in front of the horse's legs – legs thickly wrapped in rags of cloth bound with string. He looked slowly up.

A skirt at knee level, very thick, black and shiny – a leather skirt. Then metal, as he looked up further, hoops and crescents of metal. And a face, pale as the moon, looking down at him from the black sky – a face framed in a shape that he recognized: a helmet, his helmet.

He reached up and took the hand that was held down to him, pulled himself with a sucking sound out of the mud.

The person who had helped him up was about his own height, and was in a suit of ancient-looking armour. It might have been a girl or a boy, but he decided it was a girl – it was something about the fierceness of the mouth and eyes that reminded him of Maudie. But it was a very foreign face, Olly wasn't exactly sure where-foreign, but somewhere pretty far away. And pretty long ago. "Are you a Scythian?" he asked.

The girl laughed softly, let go of Olly's hand and turned towards a small rough-looking

167

pony with hard black eyes. "Do I look like a Scythian?" she said.

"I don't know," Olly said. "I suppose so."

"Well then." She took hold of the pony's plaited bridle. "We shall walk."

Then there came such booming and banging, and amongst it zipping, crackling, skirling and howling, that Olly thought his eardrums would cave in. Light, red and yellow and white, cracked open the black sky in blinding bursts.

There was another moment's lull, and the Scythian pointed ahead, to where there seemed to be a streak of faint light on a far-off horizon. Calmly she said, "That is the place. Do you have what you found?"

Olly's hand automatically went to his back trouser-pocket. "I've got the Book," he said. "But where are we?"

He had to wait a little for the stranger to reply, because there was another long burst of deafening noise.

"You know where," she said. "This is the battle."

"Which battle?" Olly asked.

"The battle that is being fought," the Scythian replied. "The battle that is always being fought when there's nothing to make it stop."

"This is where Ronald Ewart was killed, isn't it?" Olly said.

"You are safe," the girl said. "The lances and arrows would pass through you as if made of air."

"Lances and arrows," Olly snorted. "Get real, can't you?" He would have felt a lot safer face down in the mud again.

But the stranger walked calmly on. Somehow Olly trusted her and kept walking too. They went on bare mud – no grass, no trees except where now and again a stump, splintered and shivered by shell-blast, loomed up ahead and fell mournfully behind. Olly began to make out other details – coils of barbed wire, sharp stakes set at threatening angles in the ground, blast-craters, lonely lumped shapes in the mud that he guessed were dead men.

The horizon where they were headed crept closer. The light that hung there was very faint, but it reminded him, strangely, of distant sunlight.

"What are we going there for?" he asked his companion.

"We are not so much going there, as going back," she replied. "There is a woman. You must give her what you found. She can't get back without it, and she must get back."

Suddenly whips and javelins of hot energy came whizzing and scorching round their legs, while a crackling, loud yet also remote, broke out to either side of them. "Hey! They're firing on us!" Olly exclaimed.

"We are nearly there," the girl said steadily. "Don't look back."

The phantom bullets shrieked and seared around them, through them, burning yet harmless. Olly would rather have run, but the girl and her pony never altered their pace.

Soon they were climbing, and little by little Olly realized they were leaving the battle behind them. The golden light was ahead, baffling in the gloomy night.

Finally they were at the top of the hill, and a new scene stretched before them, as warm and light-filled and peaceful as the scene behind them had been dark and frightening. It was familiar-looking country – country of farm and woodland and pasture, a valley land with hills on either side notched with stony outcrops and small groups of trees – but nowhere that he recognized. At the foot of a green slope ahead of them, he saw a cottage.

It was like a house from a story, with smoke rising from a chimney just the way smoke should, whitewashed walls and russet roof tiles and tiny gleaming windows. In front were some small trees laden with creamy-white blossom.

The Scythian looked dirty and scruffy in this green country, and Olly was suddenly reminded of Amanda Sharpe, though his new companion was far dirtier. She nodded ahead.

"Don't be long." Deliberately, she turned off the path.

Olly continued on his way. Presently he reached the house, then heard voices, and coming round a corner saw an open door that led into a shady room with a stone-slabbed floor. His eyes grew used to the light and he saw that it was a kitchen, with a large table and a man sitting at it while a woman stood talking to him. He went straight in; then he stopped and looked around him wonderingly, because the kitchen was exactly the same as the kitchen at Lingerton.

He had recognized May's voice straight away. Both she and the man turned to look at him, and May stopped speaking. The man squeaked his chair back a little. He was a young man, with an open, friendly face. It was hard to tell if it was the same face that Olly had seen in the photograph, but he knew it would be Ronald Ewart.

"Well, my angel, what is it?" May said.

This startled Olly, but when May immediately went on, "Are you hungry?" he realized "angel" was just a pet name. May thought he was one of the twins. For a moment he hesitated, not knowing whether to act like one of them or whether to be himself. But then almost automatically he took the Book out of his back pocket and held it out to May; as she took it, he knew that he would say only what he had

171

to. He had no choice.

She seemed to recognize the Book, and gave a slight start. "Where did you get this from?" she asked.

"You left it behind when you came here," Olly answered. "You should have brought it with you. You can't get back without it."

"Away you go," she said abruptly. "Your sister's waiting for you."

Olly followed her eyes as she glanced out of the window, and saw a girl and a pony and a small black dog out in a meadow that sloped down from the garden of the cottage. The girl was one of the twins – the twins as young as they had been on his first occasion at Lingerton. The pony was like Polka, but it also reminded him of the Scythian's pony. The girl was trying to scramble onto its back, but the dog would bark just at the crucial moment, and the pony would move a couple of steps and she would slither off. Ronald Ewart laughed.

Without another word, Olly went outside again, but just as he got into the sunlight, he heard an exclamation, like a sob, from May. "Oh Ronald, my dearie!" He stopped. There was a short silence, then May's voice again. "Now I'm feared – I'm so feared. Hold me."

Then Olly remembered the conversation between Maudie and Uncle Marty after they had shown old Ronnie the Book, and slowly he began to understand. Everything round here was like Lingerton – and yet not quite like it: it was more as though it had been copied from the real thing, but not perfectly copied. Or perhaps it was nicer than the real thing... The light, the green-gold light of May...

This was a place of memory and imagination. Everything was as May wanted it to be: a kitchen exactly like the kitchen at Lingerton, "her kitchen" that no one could enter without her permission, but the house was the little house of her own where she would live happily ever after with her true-love Ronald. And they would have children of their own – the first would be called Ronald after his father – but the twins would always be with her too, and they would never grow up, but would be out roaming the fields and hills with their pony and their dog, coming in from the endless May sunshine only to eat the good food May had prepared for them, or to sleep. It was everything that May would never have.

It was too much – too sad. Olly couldn't stand the sadness. Why did things have to be as they were? He swallowed. "It doesn't matter," he whispered to himself. "It's all long ago anyway. It's all past." Yet it did matter.

He moved on along the path from the house, stumbling a little because his vision was blurred, and presently came face to face with the Scythian and her pony.

Soon they were toiling up the hill at the side of the valley again, and Olly could see the sky visibly darker ahead of them. May-time was unchanging in this valley, but outside it the battle and the night went on.

"May had seen the Book before," Olly said.

"Of course. How else could all this have been possible?" The girl gestured to the peaceful landscape about them.

"Anyway," Olly said, "I gave it to her."

"She'll have to be given it again," the girl said.

"How do you know that?"

"We are completing the loop; it is only half complete," she said.

"Who'll give it to her? She's already got it."

"The angel will give it to her."

"I thought that was me," Olly said.

"Yes, you are the messenger!" she laughed. And suddenly Olly knew by the weight in his pocket that the Book – somehow – was still there.

"What's going on here?" he demanded.

"You have to go backwards till you return to the starting point," the Scythian said. "So the loop is completed. When the loop is completed, the Book can be read. Do you understand? The Book joins itself to those who can help. It wishes only to be read. The woman would never have been able to read it, but she could help it to be read. That's why you must

174

go backwards, and that's why you must find her twice – once to bring her home again so that you can find what you're looking for; twice to send her out so that you can meet her here. Perhaps you are the one who will read the Book. For now, you are only the angel – but perhaps you will be the one."

And so they reached the top of the hill, and they were on a clear-cut ridge between the green-gold light on the one side and the darkness on the other. Gradually the guns fell silent, and in silence Olly and the girl went on, while he chewed over her difficult words. The light from the valley laid open their way before them, and yet made it appear more desolate, and themselves more lonely. Except for the faint swishing of the pony's tail and the thud of its feet, there was silence. It seemed to Olly that neither of them liked the silence, but neither broke it.

Presently a third valley, rough and heathery, opened up ahead of them, spreading downwards in a V from the centre of the ridge. The May valley and the valley of night were forced apart. The new valley was shrouded in grey twilight.

The Scythian stopped. "The path is too narrow here," she said. "One of us must go on, and one of us must turn back. Which will you be, the going-on one or the going-back one?"

175

Olly said nothing. He didn't know what to say. But the strangest thing about the situation was how familiar it was. It was like the two little girls – the twins – playing in the field with Polka. *Which will you be, the going-on one or the going-back one?*

He shrugged. "You choose." Or... With a sudden, sickening dread, he thought of those same two little girls thirty-five years later. One went on, one died. *Which will you be?*

Hastily he said, "I'll be the going-on one."

The girl smiled. "Goodbye then, my twin," she said, and mounted her pony and turned it round to face the sun, which just at that moment had risen over the ridge and shone fully into Olly's eyes, blinding him.

He turned away, and followed the narrow path downhill into the V-shaped valley, back into the twilight.

Before long, the rough ground became a field. He recognized it at once. Ahead, and slightly to the right, was Baldinnie – not the new Baldinnie, with the pub and the modern houses, but Baldinnie from Lingerton days – and over to his left was Lingerton itself in its shroud of bright leaves. He saw cattle wandering across a ridged field of brown soil. It was early in the morning, and cold and dewy, with the sun just rising.

He smiled, and thought he almost understood. Those cows shouldn't be on the ploughed field: they had escaped from the farm close. They should have been on their way to the Whitsun market in Edenbridge by now. It was that morning. The Scythian had talked about him going backwards; she meant backwards in time – back to the starting point, the morning when the Book had first appeared in the real world. Down in the wood ahead of him, with the dark of pine trees and the brilliant green of the big beech tree catching the sunlight, May was waiting.

She was sitting on the ground with her back to the tree, and her leg, twisted round, was stuck fast in a hole. He saw her eyes were closed as he came towards her, but the sunlight touched her face just at that moment and she opened them, squinting up at him against its rays. She said to him, "Are you an angel?"

Olly wanted to reply that he wasn't, but he knew nothing could be changed. He and May were long ago in the past, and the past was a written book, not a book with blank pages.

He reached into his back pocket, and again drew out the Living Book. "You can do anything with this," he said. "It will take you wherever you want to go."

Without a word May reached up and for a second time took the Book. This time she started leafing through its pages. Then she said, "I cannae read it."

"I know," Olly said. "But it won't matter, you'll see."

"Who does it come from? Does it belong to the Lord God?" she said.

"I can't tell you where it comes from," Olly said with a short laugh. "You'll put it in the loft. But you should keep it a while first – to get where you want to go, and then to get back."

"Very well," May replied gravely. "I'll do that."

And everything was fading. The heat beat on his back, but it was not the heat of the early morning sun: it was the heat of fire. He was lying on the ground, with his cheek pressing a young nettle plant into damp black soil and the vile smell of burning plastic in his nostrils...

MAKING EVERYTHING RIGHT

Old Ronnie had had a fit and knocked over his cooking stove, which had set fire to the caravan, which had caused a gas explosion. It was the kind of accident that everyone had been dreading for ages, and now it had happened. Ronnie wasn't hurt; he had been unconscious through the whole thing, and they had quite a job persuading him that he couldn't just go back and get on with his life. They had to show him the burnt-out caravan and the red gas-bottle stuck up in the beams where the force of the explosion had blown it.

Maudie was the one who got hurt, but she was also the hero of the hour. Uncle Marty and Jim Sharpe had gone racing up to Miglo Hall as soon as they heard the bang, and they had been just in time to see Maudie dragging the old man out of the main door – Maudie with her hair all frizzed close to her head and her face and arms black, except for where angry red splodges of burnt skin had blistered through. Uncle Marty told the tale over and over again in the weeks that followed – how he had gone on in for Olly, and found him crawling about on his hands and knees slapping his bottom and moaning *"It's gone, I've lost it! It's gone!"* and then how he had got him outside just in time to hear Maudie gasping, through terrible dry coughs, *"I think ... aha, aha ... fires are ... aha ... so cool!"* "What a pair!" he would say. "I'm telling you, man, it was like – wild, you know?"

Maudie was in hospital for two weeks, so she missed all her exams. Olly, who had been in the safest place he could be – lying on the ground in a good draught of fresh air – was let out after two days, though Ronnie was kept in for a little longer.

Olly was devastated by the loss of the Book. He had been so certain it would simply appear back in his pocket as it had done before. He lay gazing blankly at the hospital ceiling while tears of frustration poured out of the corners of his eyes and ran into his ears. He didn't try to dry them. His ears could fill up, for all he cared. The Book was gone. They had found it, he had lost it. His vision of the future, of Hill of Service Estate all full of people working towards something – something splendid,

180

connected with the Book – was now impossible. Perhaps if he had told Uncle Marty about it they would have been more careful and kept the Book somewhere safer.

He only saw Uncle Marty once for a few minutes to speak to. As soon as he tried to speak, the tears started spurting out of his eyes. "I'm sorry, Uncle Marty!" he wailed. "I'm sorry, I didn't mean it..."

"What, kiddo?" Uncle Marty looked perplexed. "What didn't you mean?"

Olly had been meaning to apologize for losing the Book and for not telling him about the vision, but other words came out. "For those things I said!" he bawled. "I didn't mean them – they weren't true."

Uncle Marty seemed genuinely surprised. He took Olly's hand and tried to make soothing noises. He was still doing that when Olly's parents came in to help him pack his things for going home, so Olly never got the chance to finish his list of apologies.

He saw Maudie briefly just before they left. She was still very hoarse, and hadn't to move her face, so she couldn't say much. Olly stared at her seared, livid skin, and a surge of pity and sadness went through him. Maudie had been pretty. He had never realized that before. But would those marks ever heal – would she not be scarred and ugly now for the rest of her life?

He was already feeling raw; the sight of Maudie set him off into a fresh bout of tears.

"Stop it!" Maudie croaked. "Idiot..."

"You were so brill, Maudie," Olly whispered.

Maudie held up a bandaged hand, waving him to stop. "Had to," she gasped. "'Cause of what I did before. Had to make everything right, OK?"

"Maudie, I've got to tell you," Olly said. "The Book's gone. This thing happened..."

Quickly, he told her about crossing the battlefield and May's secret cottage.

Maudie croaked, "Got the sack ... Lingerton ... Aunt Rosie said..."

"That's right," Olly said, after he had thought what she meant. "May and Great-Grandma Jane didn't get on too well at the end of the Lingerton days. She must have been, like, living in two places at once – in the real world and that other place. No wonder she got the sack. What am I going to do about the Book, Maudie?"

Maudie was shaking slightly. Otherwise she was lying very still, with her eyes shut. It was odd; it made Olly think of the way you shake when you're trying not to laugh. "What is it? What's wrong?" he asked.

"Idiot," Maudie whispered. "Idiot..."

Just then a nurse came in and told Olly he was making Maudie talk too much, so he was left wondering.

*   *   *

His parents drove him home, complaining bitterly all the way about Maudie's stupidity in missing her exams and risking her life for an old halfwit in a caravan. Olly tried not to listen. Later his mother phoned Aunt Rosie from the phone box, and when she came back she told Olly, rather grudgingly, that Marty had asked him to call him at Aunt Rosie's as soon as possible.

Uncle Marty was roaring with laughter even as he picked the receiver up. "Is that you, Olly?" he bellowed. "Hey – did your sister call you an idiot, by any chance?"

"Yes, she did," Olly told him. "Why?"

"'Cause you are one!" he howled. "And so am I! Maudie's the only one with any wits here!"

"Wha–what? How?" Olly stammered.

"Because it's right here," Uncle Marty explained, still guffawing away. "Exactly where it should be – stuck up in that place in Ma's garage!"

"The Book?"

"Of course! It's a loop, right? It goes round and round the loop. You gave it to May, she left it in the loft, your granny Olive pushed it through the crack, you come along and find it – round and round, just like old Ronnie's tree!"

"I am an idiot…" Olly murmured.

"Tell you what though," Uncle Marty went on, "it doesn't just go round and round exactly the same. You can read it now."

"What? You're joking! You mean there's stuff on the pages now?"

"Stuff on the pages, kiddo, as you say."

"What does it say?"

"Well, that's a problem. It's just little stacks of straight lines – just, you know, a couple of centimetres wide, neat little piles. Whole lines and broken lines – it's not even a foreign language, you know? Just lines. But hey, listen, have you ever heard this before?"

> *You are half-seen,*
> *You are in confusion.*
> *Your day comes; your page can be read:*
> *You laugh for joy.*

"Oh yes," Olly replied. "I've heard that one before."

"You know what?" Uncle Marty went on, brimming over with excitement. "Those German words down the sides of that embroidery, *ganz* and *gebrochen* – well, *gebrochen* means 'broken', right enough, but *ganz* can mean two things. It can mean 'whole' as well as 'quite'. You see? *Whole* and *broken*. The words didn't mean that the guy was gutted, like we thought: they were describing one of the combinations of whole and broken lines in the Book. And guess what? I've found the same combination – it's on page twenty-three: *broken, whole, whole, broken, broken, broken.* You see? And the one on the other side's a couple of pages on. But it's like ... it's like a code, or something..."

Olly stood, rooted to the pavement, fiddling with the ten pence coin he had left over from the phone call. He felt elated, angry at himself for not having worked out where the Book would be – and, above all, bewildered. Why couldn't the Book be read? Hadn't the Scythian said *it only wishes to be read*? Well then, why did it make it so difficult? Maybe it had to be put round the loop again, and then these stacks of lines would turn into words. But somehow he knew that wasn't right. It was the way the Scythian had spoken: twice was the number. The first time round the Book was half-seen; the second time you could see it properly. They had got all they would get.

Cars swished by, women with prams grumbled their way round him. He looked down at the coin in his hand. Funny thing, coins. Heads or tails. Only two possibilities. Forwards or back. Alive or dead. Whole or broken...

To read your life in its lines. Where had he heard that before? The scrap of paper. Was that what that embroidered text was? Could the poem have been written by somebody who had read *his* life in the lines? And did that make the lines on page twenty-six mean something?

185

Forlorn, with no belonging... That was a bit like the Whitmans too – they'd been a bit forlorn when Maudie burned the house and they lost all their belongings. The Sharpes too – they'd stood to lose everything, till Uncle Marty had come along with his lottery money and made them laugh for joy. Yet the guy who'd written the poem hadn't known anything about the Sharpes or the Whitmans. Completely different things had probably happened in *his* life – yet it could still be the same situation: you could be forlorn with no belonging in all kinds of different ways.

Maudie came home. Her face was still a mess, though the skin was healing. But her sixteenth birthday had passed while she was in hospital, and she could make her own decisions now, and she had decided she wasn't going to go back for plastic surgery. "I'd rather be ugly and useful," she said. Their mother was horrified, but there was an even bigger shock a couple of days later, when Maudie went up to the school and signed herself out.

"What's got into you?" Mrs Whitman screamed. "You've got no qualifications. What'll you do with your life? How'll you ever get a job?"

"I've got a job," she answered smartly. "I'm off back to help them build old Ronnie's new place."

"What? What new place?" their mother wanted to know.

"Uncle Marty's doing up the turret-room at Miglo Hall for him. It's to be like a bed-sit, with a solid-fuel stove, and a generator for electricity. It's all Uncle Marty's idea. It'll be really cosy for him, and a lot safer."

"Well, that's all very nice," their mother said, "but I don't see why you have to get involved in it. Are you getting paid for it?"

Maudie shrugged. "How should I know?"

"Well, a young girl who takes a job has to at least find out if she's getting paid for it," their mother argued. "In fact, it's perfectly plain to me that this is just some notion of your head-in-the-clouds uncle, and you're not going, so that's it."

"Just try and stop me," Maudie grinned. By the end of the week she had packed her bags and gone.

GREAT POSSESSION

Uncle Marty had been right about old Ronnie:
ever since the day when they had shown him
the Book he had been back to his old self. The
fire and the loss of his caravan had put him
neither up nor down. In fact, it wasn't just
Uncle Marty's idea to build him a bed-sit; old
Ronnie had been staying with the Sharpes, and
he had made such a nuisance of himself "helping" them that they had practically gone down
on their knees and begged Uncle Marty to
think of something they could do to get them
out from under their feet. That was when
Uncle Marty had suggested "Project Ronnie"
in the turret. Of course, the Sharpes could
hardly refuse Uncle Marty anything now, and
they all offered to muck in and help – as long
as they could get all the building work finished
before hay-time.

Olly, meanwhile, was helping his parents

with the move to their new house, which felt big, and so spotless he was scared to touch anything. He escaped to Fife as soon as he could at the start of the summer holidays.

Uncle Marty picked him up from Kinross. He had the Book with him, and Olly pored over it as they drove towards Rothes, and decided that the change in how it looked – with the small sharp-etched black lines swimming like tiny tadpoles on the grey-green page – exactly matched the way it felt. It was very weird: somehow it seemed not so heavy, not so full, rougher – more book-like. Had it *hatched*? It certainly looked that way.

It was just a pity that its newly hatched babies weren't easier to understand. Page after page showed only the neat little stacks of lines, whole lines, broken lines, broken lines, whole lines. Uncle Marty hadn't been able to make out any order in them.

They drove up to Miglo Hall before they went to Aunt Rosie's, and the first thing Olly saw was Maudie clambering around like a monkey on top of the turret roof.

"That's the main man in the operation," Uncle Marty said proudly. "A real Jack-of-all-trades, our Maudie. She's quite brilliant."

At eleven the next morning, Maudie finished the short roof ridge, and the main building work was complete.

"Whisky!" Uncle Marty announced, and

everyone – Maudie, Olly, Robert, Ronnie, Uncle Marty, and all seven Sharpes – had to gather in the turret-room to toast Ronnie in his new home. Mrs Sharpe and Amanda had got properly dressed up for the occasion, and Amanda looked surprisingly beautiful.

They gathered round the fireplace with its glossy new black stove and held up their plastic cups of whisky and roared "To Maudie!" because she had been such a hero, and "To Ronnie!" because it was his new home. Olly and Robert made choking faces at each other because the whisky tasted so burning. Olly glanced across the room, and saw Amanda laughing at them. He wondered if she had forgiven him for his stupid questions. He smiled at her. She smiled back.

Just then her father looked out of the window and gave an exclamation. "Who the hell's that now?" he growled. "More Social Service busybodies?"

They crowded to the window and looked out. A smart green Range Rover had appeared outside the Hall and a man in a dark suit was climbing out of it.

"Savidge," Jim Sharpe said. "Now this I willnae hae. He's just looking for some excuse to get us out of here – it's worth a lot more to him now with the new buildings..." He strode off, muttering.

A minute later he returned, looking

sheepish. "Savidge is just the driver," he said. "It's the old boy – Crooke – he's needing to speak to someone who's found a book. That'll be you, I daresay, Marty."

Olly felt his knees going a little wobbly. Someone *else* knew about the Book? "Come on," Uncle Marty called over to him, and disappeared off down the stairs.

As Olly crossed the room after him, he heard Ronnie beginning some fantastic story about how he had been the one who had phoned the lawyer. "My Auntie Betty gave me the number," he said. "I wrote it on the back of my dad's picture. It got burned. I told him I'd seen the angel but he said I had to wait till I saw the Book, so I did. But he was ill then so he didn't come. But he's here now! I thought he'd be dead. I can't speak to my Auntie Betty now. She said it would be all r—" The old man's blaring voice followed him all the way down the stairs.

Mr Crooke certainly looked on his last legs. He was a tiny, wizened old thing who lay covered in a tartan rug in the reclined front seat and spoke through the window in a thin, wheezing voice. Just as Olly came up he heard him finishing a question, "...in possession of a somewhat unusual book?"

Olly had already been a bit startled at how freely Uncle Marty talked about the Book to everyone. After what had happened with the

191

helmet, he couldn't help thinking it would have been better not to brandish it about in front of the Sharpes quite so much – not to mention old Ronnie. Now the old idiot had gone and called up this lawyer, and the lawyer would probably say it belonged to Mrs Hope or someone, and it would be taken away from them.

This time, he thought, he wasn't going to let things get out of hand. If Crooke demanded to have the book, Olly was going to take off with it! The other man, Mr Savidge, was standing some distance away contemplating the nettles. Good, that meant he would be able to make for the wood...

He turned back to Uncle Marty and Mr Crooke. Uncle Marty had already given him the thing! Old Mr Crooke's bird-like hands were fluttering over the strange pages...

"Yes," he piped, several times. "Yes. Yes. Mr Gellatly, I'll be quite honest with you, I never thought I'd see this day. I have never, in all my experience in law, received such a bizarre request from a client. But I had the highest regard for Elisabeth Hope, and this is unquestionably the book she described to me. Well, I won't waste time. I have some documents here to give you, please look through them and return them to my partners, signed, at your convenience." He handed the Book back to Uncle Marty and then picked up a large brown envelope from his lap. Uncle

Marty simply stood, gaping stupidly.

Mr Crooke gave a small wheezing laugh. "Don't worry, Mr Gellatly," he chirped. "I've had forty years to think about it – I realize it must be something of a shock for you. It was just after the death of her daughter Elspeth that Mrs Hope asked me to make certain arrangements of a very peculiar nature. They involved the finder of a particular Book, which she described to me in detail. Shortly after our last interview the fire occurred in Miglo Hall and I don't know of anyone who saw her again, though I have no reason to think that she died in the fire.

"The documents are all here, signed and witnessed, and once you've added your signature the matter will be finished. Oh, and there will be a rather fat fee which you'll have to pay to Crooke, Barbour and Savidge, but I very much doubt if that will cause you any problems."

"Sign? Witness? Fee?" Uncle Marty stumbled. "What is this? What's it all about?"

"Mrs Hope stipulated that the entire Miglo Estate – Miglo Hall, Hill of Service forest, Lower Service farm, Craigenputtock and Eastridge – as well as liquid assets running to several million pounds, should go into the ownership of the person who came to me in possession of the Book which you have just shown me."

Uncle Marty looked dazed, as if a brick had dropped on his head but he hadn't decided to be knocked out yet. "There must be some mistake," he mumbled. "Anyway, it wasn't me that found the Book, it was Olly here. Give him the bread, man."

Olly realized that shock was making Uncle Marty lapse into hippy gibberish. But he was inclined to agree, all the same. There was something a bit fishy about all this. He blushed and stepped back. "I don't want it either," he muttered.

"Can't give it to you anyway, sonny," old Mr Crooke wheezed. "It has to be the man with the Book. That's Mr Gellatly here, not you. Those were my instructions. Now, Mr Gellatly, are you going to take these papers or not?"

"No, no, man – you have to give them to Olly," Uncle Marty said, more firmly now.

"Well," said Mr Crooke, plonking the envelope back on his knee, "I'm sorry you feel that way. I can't deny I'm most disappointed, after waiting all these years. It means the estate will go to some distant relative – in the Bahamas, I think. Stinking rich as it is – they certainly don't need any more. A great pity."

This was too much for Olly. "Uncle Marty," he said, between clenched teeth.

"What?" Uncle Marty returned.

Olly thought he saw a faint smile crossing

Mr Crooke's wrinkled face. "Uncle Marty –
just take it!" he said. "It doesn't matter. You
want to see what's in that envelope, don't
you?"

"Look, I…" Uncle Marty stumbled. "Like,
it's just—"

"Jesus, just take it!" Olly shouted. He
would have kicked Uncle Marty as well, but he
felt a bit daunted by the old lawyer.

"Well?" Mr Crooke said quietly, one eye-
brow raised.

"Oh – all right then," Uncle Marty said. "It
can't hurt to look, I suppose."

"Well, thank goodness for that," Mr
Crooke sighed, and practically pushed the
envelope into Uncle Marty's hands. "Actually,
Elisabeth warned me you wouldn't be the sort
of geezer who enjoyed money," he remarked.
"The more fool you, I say. However, I think
you'll see there's a letter inside." With that, he
reached over and gave a blast on the horn
which made Olly and Uncle Marty leap back,
and which also brought Mr Savidge hurrying
over. "Time to go, David!" he called shrilly.

Uncle Marty refused to open the envelope yet.
"My nerves wouldn't stand it," he told everyone.

Later in the afternoon he took Olly, Maudie
and Robert back to his flat in Edenbridge, made
a cup of very strong coffee, settled himself in the

big armchair, and the Grand Opening took place. He fished through the documents then pulled out two sheets of fine white paper. "The letter," he said.

"*To those who have found the Living Book,*" he read out. "Those, you see? It's not just me. Oh right, listen: *In some respects I already feel I know you, even though I do not know who you are and probably never shall. It is likely that the Book will by now have given you a demonstration of its power: perhaps you have received unexpected wealth or have had an impossible wish fulfilled...* OK, baby, we're on track... Oh, whoops: *Be warned! This was ONLY a demonstration. It is not a Book which makes wishes come true!*

"*How I knew this Book was about to appear in the world again is detailed in the three journals which I have left for you in the library at Miglo Hall. They are plain black volumes with the title on the spine,* Quest For the Book, *and they will also tell you everything which I and my husband discovered in many years of travel and research – how the Book is to be interpreted and how it can be used...*

"Oh my God," Uncle Marty groaned.

"The library," Olly whispered.

"The place was burned," Maudie said.

"Go on with the letter, Dad," Robert urged.

Uncle Marty read: "*The quest for the book was the quest of our life. We have travelled to*

*many distant and inaccessible parts of the
world, in order to speak to many strange and
knowledgeable people and their knowledge
we now gladly leave to you.*

*"The first volume of our journal recounts
how a fragment of a book was discovered in
the possession of a certain German book
dealer in the last century. This fragment had
been copied from a supposedly LIVING
BOOK, about which, it was claimed, there
were many legends. The dealer said that the
copy had been made by a poet who had owned
this Living Book but who had become a
'broken man' after it was stolen from him.*

*"I was a girl of twelve then, and the frag-
ment fascinated and haunted me. It seemed to
be a love poem, and yet also something more.
I embroidered a part of it which my father had
translated and had it framed as a text, and it
has been with me all my life, until some years
ago I found I had mislaid it.*

*"I know now that loss has played a great
part in the history of the Living Book.
Strangely it appears, and then as strangely dis-
appears again. I do not believe it was stolen
from the German poet. It is plain that it does
not belong to this world, but that it comes into
the world for brief periods because it wishes to
be read – then it must return again whence it
came.*

"To my knowledge, that German poet was

the first ever to have copied the Book – and he only copied a single page of it (his copy is pasted inside the first volume of the journal). I did not understand to begin with that my text was itself not copied from the Book, but was an invention of the poet. The copy he made consisted simply of the repeated words 'ganz' and 'gebrochen'...

"Oh wow," Uncle Marty burst out, "listen to this: *What I must therefore emphasize most strongly is that you make a COPY of the Book as soon as you can. It does not stay for long! The power of the Book lies in the exact arrangement of its lines. No one who saw the Book in the past understood this. They thought the power of the Book was in the Book itself, but that is nonsense – pure superstition. The power is simply in the arrangement of the lines.*

"I do not know exactly what the Living Book's purpose is in the world, but am convinced it is for good. By making use of the information we have gathered in the journals you will no doubt discover much more, and I have no doubt you will achieve great things.

Remember us!
Elizabeth Hope, May 24th 1957."

Uncle Marty put the papers down and put his head in his hands. "Oh man," he groaned, "this is too much. This is really too much. We blew this thing. The Hopes – they spent their whole lives on this thing, and it's all gone, man, it all went up in smoke."

"Apart from that one bit of paper that dropped from the sky," Olly chanted, in a dazed kind of voice.

"The lining for a crow's nest," Uncle Marty chanted back.

There was a silence, then Uncle Marty said, "I mean, you need some kind of genius to work this out. Like, these lines – it's like a computer code, right? I mean I'm just ordinary. My life's just boring, nothing ever happens to me – it's just an ordinary, boring, stupid, waste-of-time kind of life..." He tailed off.

"Marty," Maudie said sternly, making Olly jump, because he'd never heard her leave out the "uncle" bit before, "how can you say your life's stupid and ordinary when these things have been happening to you?"

Uncle Marty glanced up at her blearily. "Yeah, but..." he said. "That's exceptional stuff. Most of it's boring and stupid. I'm not a clever guy. I can't work out codes and things..."

But something had suddenly struck Olly. "Maybe not," he exclaimed, "but we know people who can. There's a guy at my school. And – and Robert's pretty smart. Physics, and stuff. And Lucy's a really organized person – she might be great at setting up a filing system,

199

or something. Don't you see? It could all work out. There's heaps of space up at Miglo Hall. You could do up the whole place. You've got the money for it! We could get hundreds of people to come and live there; grow our own food – everything! Everyone could work on the Book together. I mean, that bit of paper – you know, the one from the sky – it said you're not supposed to keep it secret!"

Uncle Marty smiled. "Sounds brilliant, kiddo," he said. "I don't know though. These things just don't happen, you know?"

"They could happen," Olly said firmly. "They could, you know."

"Confidence of youth." Uncle Marty gave a rueful smile.

"He saw it, Marty," Maudie put in. "You saw it, didn't you, Olly? He had a vision."

"What's this?" Uncle Marty said.

"It was when he was still cross with you," Maudie explained. "That's why he didn't speak about it. But he saw it all happening, just like he's saying."

"Yeah?" Uncle Marty said. He was looking more hopeful now, but still unbelieving.

Olly shrugged. "I should have said," he mumbled. "I'm sorry. It's true though. It was all happening. You were in charge – well, Maudie was in charge really, but you were kind of in charge in charge. There was such a great atmosphere, you know? Everyone was

200

helping with everything, but you were the one who was really getting the Book sorted out. You said you had to get inside the pattern—"

"I said that?" Uncle Marty said.

"Well," Olly scratched his head, "you will, I suppose. You haven't said it yet."

"Yeah," Uncle Marty said slowly. "Yeah, you're right. I will. And you know what? I think I know where to start. Ma's old embroidery – that's the *one* clue we've got left about how you use the Book – because that old German poet guy had worked out something about how to *read his life in the lines*. You know?"

He pulled his ponytail round and examined the end of it for a long time, until his eyes became crossed. At last he said, "You know, back, like a hundred years ago, people looked at all that old Egyptian writing and they didn't know what it meant. Like, it was just hiero-glyphics. But then they found this bit of stone with some hieroglyphics on it and some Greek writing beside it. And they reckoned the Greek writing meant the same thing. And they already understood it, so they used it to work out how to read the Egyptian writing. So it's like the same thing, yeah? If we can understand what this old German dude was meaning and how it's connected to these whole and broken lines, that could be our clue to understanding the Book. Our one clue. Wow,

I mean, just think what would have happened if Mrs Hope hadn't mislaid her embroidery in Ma's hallstand! Where would it be now? Ashes, that's where. Why did she mislay it? She didn't mean to! But that's the whole thing, man. There's a *power* at work, influencing events. Not in a big way, just – little nudges, you know? *Something*, out there, that reckoned her little bit of embroidery would be all we'd need – just enough for us to get working on…"

"That's it!" Olly broke in. "That's what I couldn't get – you know, why it all had to be in code, and so difficult and that. I mean, does the Book want to be read or doesn't it? But it's obvious. The Book gives you *just enough*. Or the time ghost does, or something does. And *that's* why Miglo Hall burned down, that's why old Mrs Hope's books had to get burned. Because otherwise we'd have had *too much*. You see? If we'd had old Mrs Hope's instructions to follow, we might have been able to understand the Book without any help from anyone else."

"That would've been all right, wouldn't it?" Robert put in.

"Sure, in a way," Olly said. "But we'd have been, like, sitting up in this brilliant beautiful house that used to belong to the Hopes. Like Lord Muck, you know – we don't need anyone, and no one needs us. I don't think that's what the Book wants. That's the point. It wants everyone involved. Think about it – that's the one scrap of information we still have, out of all Mrs Hope's instructions! *The Book doesn't want to be kept secret.*"

Uncle Marty leapt up and practically hugged him. "Olly, you're a genius!" he crowed.

In fact, as they all said later, Uncle Marty was never as doubtful as he sounded: he just wanted to be persuaded a bit. He did grumble some more about not wanting to be in charge of anything, but then Maudie gave him a terrible ticking-off about how it was about time he started acting adult for a change.

That made him turn quite sensible, and that same week he took the four young people – Olly, Maudie, Robert and Lucy – down to the lawyers and got all kinds of documents drawn up. The five of them were made Trustees of the Miglo Estate, which meant they all owned the estate together but none of them could do anything unless all the others agreed about it. The Sharpes were given the tenancy of Lower Service farm for ever, rent-free, as long as the farm remained part of the Estate. Uncle Marty had to write out the biggest cheque he had ever seen and give it to Crooke, Barbour and Savidge, because Mr Savidge said that was what all the documents had cost to prepare.

"It's a drop in the ocean though," Uncle Marty said, "compared to what we've still got."

"But we've got a lot of work to do," Maudie reminded him.

Olly was the one entrusted with copying out the Book. It was not a long task, but it was more difficult than it looked. After poring over the grey-green pages for a while, the dark lines would begin to jump about in a queer fashion, and it became hard to be sure you had got the proper combinations of whole and broken lines. Every time he had finished a page he had to pass it on to Maudie and Uncle Marty to be checked.

About a week after they had read Elisabeth Hope's letter for the first time, Olly, glancing ahead, saw he had only three more pages to do. He grew excited at the thought that he had almost finished something which, apparently, no one else had ever done before: copy the Living Book out completely.

He was working in the old library of Miglo Hall, where an old card-table of Aunt Rosie's had been set up for him among the tall weeds. He had been carefully copying for the last hour, trying not to be annoyed at the flies which kept buzzing past him or landing on his writing-paper (none of them went near the Book), when all of a sudden he had the strange feeling of silence which sometimes comes when you are being watched. Without thinking, he glanced up, and found himself in the unwinking gaze of a splendid blue-black crow which was standing on the windowsill with its head on one side.

For around ten seconds the two of them, boy and crow, stared at each other; then suddenly, as if it had just thought of something, the crow made a clumsy stagger backwards and fell off the sill out of sight. Olly leaped to his feet, knocking his chair over, and ran to the window to see if the bird was all right.

Apparently it was. It struggled out of the weeds growing against the wall and went hopping in an unhurried fashion towards the forest of shoulder-high nettles that still guarded Miglo Hall. It stopped on an old broken roof slate. Then it lifted its tail up very deliberately in Olly's direction and let out a very large dropping before turning towards the sycamore wood and flapping slowly off.

Olly stared after it, and the vision he had had drifted back to him: the courtyard and the well. "The well," he murmured. "That slate marks where we've to dig the well." Immediately he made his way outside, found a rusty iron stake lying just outside the front door and went over and drove it deep into ground beside the marked slate. It felt like a job well done as he returned to the library.

There, the chair was still lying on the ground. He picked it up, and then paused, staring at the table. Where was the Book?

The writing-paper was there, white sheets covered with the endless black lines; the pencil and rubber and ruler and pen were there. No Book. To begin with he thought he must have knocked it off the table as he scrambled to his feet, but as he searched around, vainly, among the weeds, he realized that if he had knocked the Book off he would have knocked everything else off too.

Feverishly he grabbed all his sheets up, and went leaping out through the window, pelting round to Ronnie's turret-room, where Uncle Marty and Maudie were busy painting the walls, while old Ronnie sat on his gleaming new stove (not lit) and gave them advice.

"Maudie! Marty!" he gasped. "It's gone! The Book's gone! It disappeared!"

Heads turned and regarded him from the tops of ladders. Brushes were held poised. Paint dripped onto the floor. Breathlessly, Olly related what had just happened.

"Oh no," Maudie groaned.

"How much did you still have to do?" Uncle Marty wanted to know.

"Three pages!" Olly wailed. "I'll never be able to finish it now!"

There was a crack, followed immediately by a *splat*. Maudie had dropped her paint pot. "You haven't," she said. "You haven't cocked it up right at the very end."

"Is it a big cock-up, do you think?" Uncle Marty asked, in a trembling voice.

"Oh, probably not," Maudie said. "Just the difference between whether the thing works or not. Not a big difference."

But Olly's panic of a few moments ago had gone. He saw it quite clearly. Somehow, there was something utterly *right* about the way the crow had come and disturbed him at the last moment. They were in the pattern; it was all part of how the Living Book worked – with disappointment as well as with success.

Like an echo from long ago he could hear Uncle Marty's voice stumblingly reading out the words on the scrap of paper from the sky on an August morning outside Burnside House: *no despairing, no complaining, no giving up, no thought of evil things, no conflict, no battle, no doubt as to... Hey, this is my kind of thing, man.*

He smiled, rolled his eyes in an Uncle Marty-ish sort of way. "Hey, hang loose, friends," he crooned. "No one's ever copied as much as this before. So that's progress, right? We can only do as much as we can do."